REDEMPTION IN COTTONWOOD SPRINGS

A Cottonwood Springs Cozy Mystery - Book 7

BY

DIANNE HARMAN

Published by: Dianne Harman
www.dianneharman.com

Interior, cover design and website by
Vivek Rajan

ISBN: 9781086143959

CONTENTS

ACKNOWLEDGMENTS

To all of you who have struggled with substance abuse and to stay clean after a stay in prison, I wish you the best.

To all of you who have overcome whatever led to you going to prison, congratulations on making a new life.

To all of you who are going through difficult times, may they end for you and may you find happiness.

To all the people who work so hard to see my books published, please know how much I appreciate what you do.

To my readers, who make all of this possible, thank you.

And to Tom, for everything, thank you.

Win FREE Paperbacks every week!

Go to www.dianneharman.com/freepaperback.html and get your FREE copies of Dianne's books and favorite recipes immediately by signing up for her newsletter.

Once you've signed up for her newsletter you're eligible to win three paperbacks. One lucky winner is picked every week. Hurry before the offer ends!

PROLOGUE

Mike Loomis was glad he wasn't in prison anymore. He'd done his time, and now he was out, and that was all that mattered. He'd do whatever he had to do in order to stay on the straight and narrow. No more dealing, no more drugs from now on. It was going to be a clean and sober life for him. He'd come too far to go back to who he was before. Until he spent time in prison, he'd never realized just how much he'd been numbing himself from everything for all those years.

At the time he thought he needed to be numbed, but thanks to the detox and the rehab, he knew now that the only way to get over something was to go through it. No matter how many drugs you took, they could never truly take away your pain. The only thing he intended to do when winter came was go skiing again. That had been his one true passion, and he'd been good at it. Too much time had passed since he'd been able to ski down the slopes on some fresh powder. He couldn't wait until the day came that he could strap on some skis and feel the wind in his face.

He'd gotten mixed up in the drug game years ago, and he'd ended up getting busted for it. It was around the same time that Lucy, the owner of the B & B in Cottonwood Springs was murdered. Mike had known her because he'd been the handyman at the B & B.

It had been an upsetting time for the town because the victim was the then Sheriff's sister. Mike had been a suspect in the murder investigation, but he was no murderer. Although, when he looked back, he could understand why he'd been considered as a prime suspect. He'd done some pretty bad things back then and was well known to the sheriff's department.

Standing in the kitchen, he began pulling vegetables from the refrigerator, so he could make a salad. He shook his head as he realized what he was doing. There was no way he ever would have eaten a salad in the past. And that's how his life was now, before and after prison. One man had gone in and a completely different man had come out.

Washing the veggies off, he thought about how he'd managed to get a great job and a decent house to live in. Working for the city, mowing the grass at the cemetery and doing other outdoor maintenance, was a blessing. Good thing the city had a policy about helping ex-cons.

There couldn't be a better job for a guy like him. He enjoyed cutting the grass and helping to maintain the trees. Cleaning up the city streets and helping ensure that Cottonwood Springs looked nice had become important to him. Like everything else, it was something he'd only recently learned about himself. Even his yard was well maintained now, and he planned to plant a few more things in it if his landlord would allow it.

Mike had left the front door open and a nice breeze was drifting through the house. He could see the driveway that curved around the back of the house and up to the garage. He envisioned his future car sitting out there, all polished and shining in the sun. He had started saving money for a car and was really looking forward to becoming the proud owner of a nice car.

Mike knew he should probably keep his door shut and locked considering what had recently happened to him. It wasn't like he'd forgotten. How could he? Someone had broken into his house while he was asleep and left photos. He'd been pretty sure he was being followed and the pictures proved it, but since it was the middle of the day, he doubted he had anything to worry about by leaving the door open.

Besides, Sheriff Davis and Brigid were doing all they could to find out who had been following him and left the pictures. The sheriff was out of town right now, but it wasn't like he'd be gone forever. And, from what he'd heard, Brigid was just as good as he was, if not better, at solving mysteries and catching the bad guys. She'd assured him that she was on it. He just needed to take a deep breath and relax.

The sound of a vehicle startled him from his thoughts and made him look out front. It looked like a van from some sort of a cleaning company, so he went back to preparing his salad. He pulled out a cutting board and knife and started to chop the vegetables for his salad. Humming along to the song on the radio, he shook his head at his jumpiness and told himself to relax.

"You gotta' chill out, my man," he said quietly to himself. He turned up the radio so it was a little louder, relaxing into the song, and feeling his shoulders release some of their tension. There was nothing he could do now except wait and see as the investigation continued, so why spend that time filled with anxiety?

His mind ran through the faces of the different people who might be responsible for following him and the break-in. Just thinking about it made him realize he was attacking the vegetables, rather than cutting them. The more he thought about it, the more he realized that these were some very bad people that were popping up on his mental list of suspects. Or at least they were when he knew them.

He had a feeling they might think he'd ratted them out when he was in prison, but he hadn't. He'd just kept his nose clean and done what he was told and that's how he'd been able to get an early release from prison. It had something to do with his being a non-violent offender. He hadn't really cared about the reason they were letting him out early, just that he was getting out.

By then he'd been longing for air that wasn't behind razor wire so much that he dreamed about it every night. He dreamed of standing in the mountains again and feeling the breeze on his face. Camping next to a gurgling mountain stream and waking up to cook breakfast over a campfire. Those had been his dreams, and they'd kept him sane while he'd been behind bars.

He heard a noise somewhere in the house which made him pause. He turned, the knife still in his hand, suddenly feeling as though he wasn't alone. He looked around the kitchen and when he didn't see anyone, he relaxed a little. When he'd heard the sound, he'd been certain he'd turn and see someone standing there. Mike was relieved he hadn't, but now he wouldn't be able to relax until he'd thoroughly checked out the entire house.

Slowly he crept to the back door and looked around the back yard to see if anything was out of place. Sometimes the neighbor's cat knocked a pot or something over which always scared him. Satisfied nothing was different out there, he crept across the kitchen to the archway that led to the front room. Just as he was stepping across the threshold, something heavy slammed into his face.

Instantly, he saw red. The blow left his ears ringing and he nearly blacked out, but he swung out with his knife to defend himself. It caught on something, but he wasn't sure what. His attacker made a grunting noise, so he was hopeful he'd done some damage.

As his vision cleared, he saw a man standing in front of him wearing a black mask. He blinked before lunging at the attacker with his knife. This time, the person deftly avoided him. The intruder grabbed Mike's laughing Buddha statue from the nearby end table and hit his hand that held the knife. Pain radiated through his hand as he dropped the knife on the floor. He reached for it, hoping he could grab it and gain the offensive, but that wasn't the case. Instead, the person brought the statue crashing down on his head. He felt a sharp searing pain as darkness engulfed him, and he collapsed on the floor.

His attacker wasn't sure at first if he'd killed him. Mike had collapsed so fast that he was afraid he might have. Reaching down, he felt for a pulse. After a moment he found it and he relaxed. He didn't want Mike dead, anyway not yet. He had to find out exactly what he'd told the police in order to get out of prison so quickly.

It was imperative he find out if Mike had said anything that would implicate him or anyone he knew. Once he found out what information he'd given the law enforcement officials, he'd know what he was dealing with. He planned all along on killing Mike because he was a liability, but if he'd squealed, it was going to be a slow and painful death. If he hadn't, it would be fast.

He was certain Mike had told the prison officials something, and part of him wanted to just smash the statue down on Mike's head and finish him off right then and there. He doubted anyone would miss him. He raised the statue over his head to deliver the final killing blow, but then he stopped. No, he had to know exactly what he'd told them.

Mike might not tell him everything, but he desperately needed to find out everything he could. He needed to take Mike somewhere so he could question him.

Tugging off the mask he wore, he moved into the kitchen in search of something he could use to tie Mike up. That's when he saw that the driveway circled around to the back of the house. Perfect.

Rifling through some kitchen drawers, he found some fairly long zip ties. He rushed back to Mike's unconscious body and bound his hands together. That would at least keep him from doing anything if he woke up. He hurried out the front door and climbed into the driver's seat of the van. He started it up, pulled into the driveway, and circled around to the back of the house.

After he parked the van, he rushed into the house through the back door, relieved to see Mike was still lying on the floor. He wedged the door open, returned to the van, and opened the rear doors. Making sure there was room to shove Mike inside the van, he pushed a few things out of the way and returned to the house.

When he was inside, he put his arms around Mike and began to drag him out to the van. Apparently, Mike had been working out when he was in prison, because Mike was much bigger and heavier than he remembered. Still, he managed to get Mike loaded up in the van without much trouble. He shoved his legs in and slammed the doors shut.

Feeling really good about how well it had gone, he closed the back door of the house before returning to the van and climbing in. He'd have to take Mike to the abandoned building he used before he returned the van to the cleaning company. With his gloves still on, he started the van and began to back down the drive way. As he pulled onto the street, he noticed that no one was around. He was certain he'd pulled it off without a hitch.

CHAPTER ONE

Brigid and Linc were relaxing in the back yard on lounge chairs while their dogs Jett and Lucky ran around the yard chasing each other. The sun was dipping lower on the horizon and the cool autumn breeze ruffled their hair as Brigid took a deep breath.

It felt good to kick her feet up and just take a moment to do absolutely nothing. Her eyes were closed and she ran her fingers through her red hair, brushing it up and away from her neck. A slight smile played across her lips as she enjoyed the cool fresh air.

"What are you smiling about," her husband, Linc, asked. "Daydreaming about something good?"

"Not really," she said as she opened her eyes. "Just feeling grateful, is all."

"Me too," he sighed.

"It's still a little strange not having to drive Holly anywhere," she admitted. "But she seems to love the car we gave her for her birthday."

"That she does," Linc said. "You'd think she was trying to wear the tires off of it as much as she drives around town, but I'm glad she's out doing things instead of sticking around the house." Linc sat up to watch the dogs as they started to bark at each other. He chuckled while watching them play. Jett, the huge Newfoundland, was laying on the ground allowing tiny Lucky to pounce all over him.

"As long as Holly's enjoying herself," Brigid sighed. "That's the important part. I love seeing her acting like a teenager rather than a responsible adult."

Linc looked across the yard at the house next door that he'd left when he'd married Brigid, and which he still owned. He sighed.

"What's wrong?" Brigid asked, concerned. It was very rare for her husband to look across the yard at his old home which he still sometimes used as an office and appear sad. He loved the place and that was the main reason they still held onto it, despite him moving in with Brigid and Holly after he and Brigid were married.

"Rich Jennings and I were talking the other day," he began. "He mentioned something that I initially dismissed, but now I'm starting to see that it might be worth thinking about."

"Oh?" Brigid asked. She was curious now. Why would the former sheriff of Cottonwood Springs have something to say about Linc's old house? Did he know someone who might want to buy it? Maybe Linc was considering selling it.

"He was telling me how busy things had started getting with the B & B he owns. He said he advertised on a few websites, and now he's almost always got his rooms booked. Rich said since we're out here on the edge of the town, we could probably do well if we converted my house into a B & B," Linc said. "But if you don't like the idea, I understand."

Brigid looked over at the house and then back to Linc. "And this is something that you want to do?" she asked.

"Well, my first reaction was to dismiss it completely. I mean, what do we know about running a B & B? But the more I talked to Rich, the more doable it sounded. If we want to leave town, we can either find someone to watch the place or just not book it during those dates," he said.

Brigid listened carefully to what he was saying and could tell that he'd really been giving this idea a lot of thought. She considered it for a moment, then decided to point out the obvious first. "There aren't many bedrooms in it. I'd think that might be a problem for a B & B," she said.

"That's true," he nodded. "I said that to Rich. There's already two bedrooms plus the office in it. I'm thinking we could add on two or three more plus clear out some trees between here and there. Rich knows someone that would do a great job. We could make something of an outdoor area for guests. I'd put a privacy fence between our yard and my house. It would just involve some small adjustments," he said.

"I don't know. I love staying at a B & B, but I'm already pretty busy with editing and the sheriff's department work," she said as she shook her head. She liked the idea, but she had a lot on her plate as it was.

"I can do most of the work," Linc said. "I've already cut back my clients, so I could easily manage both. I'll deal with the construction that will be needed, as long as you give me input on the interior design, and all of the things you're better at than me." He was grinning so wide that even his eyes seemed to be smiling. It seemed as though he was talking himself into it as they spoke.

"If you really want to do this, you know I won't stand in your way," Brigid finally said. "I'll be behind it completely. But we have a lot of work to do before we can even think about having guests," she pointed out.

"Oh, I know," he nodded. "But Rich said he'd help out in any way he can. Then, when we're ready to take guests, he said he'd refer any that he couldn't take over to us, which would be like free advertising."

"Let's slow down just a little," Brigid chuckled. "We've got to start at the beginning."

"I know," he sighed. "I just get more and more excited every time I think about the idea. Us, having our own B & B. Who would have thought?"

"Not me," she admitted. "But I can see the draw of it." She couldn't really see herself running a B & B, but her friend Lucy had always told her how much she enjoyed meeting people from all over the country and even the world. She had one reservation. "What about when things come up? You can always plan for a vacation or something, but things do come up like family emergencies or something of that nature."

"That's very true," he said, pausing. "We could hire someone after we get up and running. Maybe part time to help with the cleaning and various things like that. We'd make sure they'd be available if something came up," he said as he brainstormed out loud.

"That could probably work. I think Rich does that, too," Brigid said. She stood up from her lounge chair and stretched. "So exactly how much thought have you put into this?" It seemed he'd done a lot more than just slightly thinking about the idea.

"I've been considering the idea for a few days," he admitted. "But I wasn't going to say anything until I'd thought it through. Otherwise, why talk about it? But the more I thought about it, the more I liked the idea."

"Can I think about it for a while?" she asked. "I don't plan on being a deal breaker, but I would like to spend a little time with the idea and mull it over. You know, look at it from all the different angles."

"Absolutely," he said with a nod. "But do you mind if I look into how much it will cost to add on to my house while you're thinking about it? I won't set anything in motion until you give me the green light," he promised.

"That's fine. Thanks," Brigid said. Just the way he was handling this was one of the reasons why she loved him so much. He was so kind and considerate when it came to her. She never felt bullied into anything, which was exactly what her ex had done. "You talk to and do whatever it is you need to do. I'll be interested to see how much this will cost us up front," she said with a raised eyebrow.

"I've got a decent nest egg built up that should cover most of it," he said. "I'm starting to lean towards just adding on two more rooms. That would leave more money for the decorating and the outdoor stuff. It would also leave room for adding even more eventually. That is, if we enjoy it and do well."

"Sounds like a smart idea," she agreed. "I'm going to head inside and get ready for dinner. Jett, Lucky," she yelled to the dogs. "Let's go inside."

"Okay, babe. I'll be in there in just a few," he said as he stood up. "I think I'm going to go over to my house and look around. Just to see how much would need to be changed."

"Sounds good," she said as she leaned over and kissed him. "Take all the time you need."

As she headed inside with the dogs, she began to imagine what it would be like if she was cooking breakfast for a group of guests at the B & B. When she imagined sharing conversation with interesting strangers or even possibly having one help her cook, it did seem intriguing. After all, how many times had she stayed at a B & B and offered to help? It was part of the charm of a B & B. You had human interaction you didn't get at a hotel or motel.

When she got to the kitchen, she began to pull things out of the cabinets as she continued to daydream. The more she thought about it, the more interested she became. She was a little concerned about Holly and how she'd feel about it. She'd definitely ask her when she came home, but the truth was she'd probably only be living with them another handful of years. But then there was the question if Brigid would want to be tied down like that once Holly was gone.

She remembered what Linc had said about hiring someone, but she was just being realistic. They'd both be worried about their guests while they were away. Whoever they hired would have to be extremely trustworthy for Brigid to be able to leave something as important as their business in their hands.

Lucky trotted into the kitchen and laid down under the table, panting from all the playing he'd done outside. Brigid looked over to see that Jett had already climbed up on the old loveseat that he called his own and started napping. Before she started dinner, she topped off their water bowls, in case they decided they needed a drink.

That's when she thought about their pets. How would they feel about all the people next door if it was converted into a B & B? Granted, it wasn't like they were going to have a lot of traffic, but that didn't mean all the different people might not bother them.

But as she started chopping some lettuce for a salad, she realized just how much Jett loved people. He was like a dog version of Linc. Always happy to make a new friend and try something new. Perhaps they could even make their B & B pet friendly?

So many people were taking their furry family members on vacation with them these days. That seemed to be what really made it possible in her mind, having a pet friendly policy would probably be a big boost to business. Happily, she continued to daydream, fairly certain she'd already made up her mind.

CHAPTER TWO

Jesse Stanford was used to doing things his way. He wasn't a very big man, but he made up for it in sheer power. He'd been lifting weights and building up his physical prowess ever since he became involved in illegal activities.

It didn't do a man any good to try to be a leader if he didn't have an intimidating appearance. As time went on, he found he was actually quite good at being a drug kingpin of sorts. He contributed the majority of his success in that endeavor to the popularity of his club. After all, what better place to sell drugs than a night club?

All the customers were already there buying his watered-down booze. Jesse had just made sure they could take care of all their vices in one place. Kind of one-stop shopping. It was a simple case of supply and demand, and with time, he'd risen to the top.

There had been many people over the years who had threatened to shut him down. People who thought of themselves as heroes would confront him about his operations and think their idle threats were something he'd actually be concerned with.

But Jesse had enough money now that he wasn't concerned. He'd built too solid of a foundation for it to be rocked by idle threats. Keeping his employees happy was one of the keys to him sitting so confidently on his throne. Happy people don't go running their mouths off to the cops or bite the hand that feeds them.

He sat in his office at the club looking over the plans for a second club he was thinking about opening. He'd spread everything across his large wooden desk, allowing him to see all the pieces at once. Jesse was still debating if he wanted to build the new club here in Denver or if he wanted to expand his reach and build it in another town.

In other words, should he build his mountain higher or spread out? That was the question. It was a tough call and one he'd been mulling over for a few days now. He was worried the wrong choice might mean his business would start to flounder, or worse. He was also very aware that he could always be caught by the law.

He leaned back in his oversized leather chair, weighing his options once again. If he stayed in Denver for his next project, potentially he could be hurting himself. If he had two locations in the same town, would his current club suffer because of it?

The location he was contemplating was in a more upscale area. He could put out all the money to build and advertise it, only to find his regular customers didn't like going to that part of town and the people who did live there might not find it to their taste. This was his thinking and why he was leaning towards opening it in another town.

There were much smaller, but still very substantial, towns nearby that could potentially have the clientele for one of his clubs. The more he thought about it, the more he leaned in that direction. Along with his drug ring in the club, he had numerous dealers in other locations.

Even the smaller towns usually had someone who was willing to travel to him. Some guys really surprised him with the amount of product they could move in these little towns. He figured there wasn't much else for them to do there. After all, when the town's biggest attraction is a bowling alley and a park, what do you expect the residents to do? Knit? As he began searching online through property listings, as he had done regularly during the last few days, there was a knock on his office door.

"Yes?" he called out. He didn't like being interrupted when he was thinking, and these days it seemed that was the only time people needed him.

One of his employees, Jose, entered the office and shut the door behind him. He was a small man with deep set beady eyes, a man who kind of made himself invisible, but that seemed to make him good at knowing what was going on around the club. He'd become something of a spy for Jesse. "You remember how you wanted to know if anyone who used to work for us ended up in prison? And remember that guy, Mike Loomis, who ended up in the slammer?" Jose asked.

"Yes, I remember," Jesse said with a nod. "What's your point?" Jose didn't always have intel that was pressing, so Jesse was hoping he'd just spit it out and let him get back to his deliberation.

"Well, I just heard that Mike got out not too long ago, which is a lot earlier than he was expected to be released," Jose pointed out. He nervously looked down at his feet and the black carpet with golden sunbursts on it.

"Is that so?" Jesse asked, finally looking up from his computer. "And has he reached out to us to start working again?"

The man shook his head. "Not a peep. I heard Alfie ran into him and brought it up, but Mike said he didn't want to do it anymore."

A shiver ran through Jesse's body, but he didn't let Jose see it. It was definitely not good news to hear that one of your former dealers wants out.

"Did he give a reason why he doesn't want to run some product anymore? Or why he was able to get out of prison early?" he questioned.

Jose shook his head. "Nope. Alfie said he seemed kind of

nervous. Kept saying he had somewhere to be."

"Hmm," Jesse said, nodding. "See what else you can find out. He needs to be tailed, so we know if he's talking to the law. I want to hear about every move he makes, even what he's eating for dinner, you understand? That kind of surveillance. We need to know if he's a threat, because if he's coming after me, he's coming after all of us, got it?"

"Yeah, I got it, boss," Jose said. "I'll ask around, and we'll set up a plan to watch the guy. What do you want me to do if it looks like he's up to no good?"

"Let me know. Don't make any moves without my approval. I want to make sure it's done right if we do have to deal with him. If he's running his mouth off to the law, they'll be watching him. Don't let anyone get sloppy."

"I understand," Jose said with a nod before he slipped out of the office. Once the door latch clicked into place, Jesse stood up and began to pace.

If Mike Loomis got out early, he thought, *that can't mean anything good. Most likely he snitched on someone to shorten his sentence. Or, he plans on setting someone up. Someone who's a much bigger fish, like me.*

The more he thought about it, the more worried he got. He decided that Mike Loomis was a liability. The only way he could think that Mike had been able to get released this early meant that he'd already given law enforcement information or that they planned on using him to take down someone bigger than him.

Jesse couldn't see it happening any other way. As far as Jesse knew, the guy hadn't associated with anyone else but him when he was involved in drugs, which wasn't good. He had a feeling that preventative measures would need to be taken.

The fact of the matter was, though, he didn't know just how much he needed to worry. He couldn't plan a course of action until he had all the facts. Jesse didn't get to where he was without being smart in his dealings. There was a reason people followed him, and a reason why they also obeyed him. No one crossed him and walked away from it, or there would be repercussions.

He knew enough to start putting things in place to deal with Mike. If Mike was thinking about talking, the right motivation might convince him to keep his mouth shut. He walked back to his desk and retrieved his cell phone from beneath all the papers strewn across it. He typed a text message telling one of his trusted men he wanted to see him as soon as possible. As always, he responded immediately and said he'd be there shortly.

That's what Jesse liked to hear, and that's why Luis Lopez was so trusted. Jesse knew that Luis would never turn on him. Good men like Luis were hard to find, which was why Jesse knew it was important to keep him happy. He wasn't sure what he'd do without him. After they arranged a meeting, Jesse slid his phone into his pocket and turned toward the large one-way window that overlooked the dance floor of his club.

He felt overwhelmed with all the different things that were running through his mind at the moment. Fear had him imagining the police bursting through his front doors and trashing the place. If they came through the doors with a search warrant, he knew he'd be screwed. He wasn't sure just how much illegal stuff was in the building right now, but there was no doubt that enough was here that he'd be arrested.

As Jesse looked over the crowd with his imagination running wild, he shook his head and closed his eyes, trying to clear his head. When he opened his eyes again, he was able to focus more on what was really happening and not let his mind get hung up on the "what ifs."

The club was almost filled to capacity tonight, which meant money rolling into his bank account. People were dancing and drinking their cares away, and what was the point of owning a club if you couldn't have a little fun now and then, just like his patrons were? He resigned himself to the fact that he couldn't do anything about Mike Loomis tonight, and his men needed some time to find out what exactly was going on with him.

Patience, to a certain extent, was key here. He'd know soon enough what Mike Loomis was up to. Jesse decided he might as well have a little fun in order to distract himself. He took off his suit jacket and tossed it on the couch before loosening his shirt. Tonight, was going to be his night to celebrate making it in this world. He was glad that he'd spent extra time at the tanning salon, because the ladies always enjoyed his body more when he was darker.

He stepped out of his office and nodded at one of his employees who was walking by as he undid his shirt cuffs. He rolled them up and jogged down the stairs as the music thumped and the lights flashed. Stepping into the crowd Jesse began to dance to the music as he made his way toward the bar.

He wanted a nice stiff drink from one of the bottles beneath the bar, the ones that weren't watered down. While he was watching the bartender pour his drink, a young woman bumped into him and then smiled. She turned and began dancing in front of him, her dark purple hair shining in the lights. Jesse smiled, maybe he didn't need that drink after all.

CHAPTER THREE

Brigid and Holly had taken a trip to the mall for the day and were enjoying strolling past the various shops and taking their time. They didn't have any specific thing they were shopping for, but it was more of a chance for them to get out of the house and spend time together. So far, they'd talked about anything and everything that had come to mind, not only while they were at the mall, but on the drive into the city as well.

"I can't make my mind up what I want to do for a career," Holly admitted as they stepped into a trendy clothing store. There was loud music playing, which Brigid wasn't quite sure should actually be considered music, but the clothes were attractive. Holly really liked the store, otherwise Brigid would have immediately turned around and gone elsewhere.

"You don't have to decide right now," Brigid said. "And I know this isn't what they tell you in school, but college isn't the be-all, end-all. There are some amazing jobs out there that don't even require a college degree." She watched as Holly pulled out a loose white top and considered it before she put it back and reached for a black version.

"I've heard that," Holly said. "But since I don't know what I want to end up doing, I can't decide what road I should take. I don't want to go through all the trouble of applying for scholarships, then go to college, and when I'm finished, change my mind. That would be a waste of time," she said with a sigh. She put the black top back and then moved over to a rack that held jeans.

"Well, do you have a list of things that interest you?" Brigid asked. "That might give you a starting point."

"Kind of," Holly admitted as she looked around with a frustrated look. "I think I'm done at this store. See anything that looks interesting?" she asked.

Brigid shook her head. "This place is nice, but it's not really my style," she said. They left the store and began walking, looking in store windows as they did so. Brigid was glad to leave the rhythmic thumping of the music behind them.

"Well, I've considered law enforcement work," Holly began. "Because of obvious reasons. But I've also been looking at art school, although I don't really think I have the talent for that," she said as she eyed a kiosk that sold pretzels. "I've also been considering nursing, psychology, and even starting my own business."

"You really are all over the place with this," Brigid said with a chuckle. She understood, though. There had been a time in her life when she'd been unsure of what direction she wanted to go when it came to making a career choice.

"Pretty much," Holly said, looking forlorn. "I guess I probably should narrow it down," she confessed with a heavy sigh.

"Probably," Brigid agreed. "Well, first, I think law enforcement work is a good one to have on your list. You obviously like to solve mysteries, and you're good at it, but do you enjoy it?" she asked.

"Yeah, I do," Holly said as she nodded. "I like knowing that I made a difference and helped someone. Plus, I really like the part where you're looking for clues and trying to find out who the culprit is. It's like a puzzle or something you're trying to solve."

"Then it should definitely be on your list of possibilities," Brigid agreed. "It seems like you're a natural at it. Nothing wrong with at least keeping it in mind. What was the next one? Art school? Because you like to draw, right? I think you're really talented."

"Right and thanks," Holly said with a smile. "When I'm drawing, it takes me out of my head for a little while, you know?"

"Yes, but how often do you make time to draw?" Brigid asked. She knew the answer, but wanted Holly to think about it.

"Not very often," Holly said. "Which probably isn't a good sign, is it?"

"It's not bad," Brigid began. "But if you're going to spend money and go to school to learn to do something, you might want to make sure it's really your passion and not just a hobby. And there's nothing wrong with having a hobby you love. It's just that at your age it's key to figure out what's a passion and what's just a hobby."

"That makes sense," Holly said, nodding. "But that kind of test seems harder to use when it comes to some of my other choices." She looked forlornly through the window of a restaurant.

"That's true," Brigid confessed. "Nursing is hard work and long hours, but you could work in a hospital, nursing home, or even visit people in their homes. However, you need to consider that there's a lot of nasty stuff you'd probably have to deal with," she pointed out.

"I know, which is why it's slipping lower on my list. I like working with people, but I kind of don't like gross stuff. I'm not so sure my stomach could handle it," she chuckled. "I've been reconsidering that profession. Especially after career day when the nurse who came to talk to us really laid it all out. You know, what she has to do on a regular basis."

"What I'm hearing is that your list is made up of a bunch of things you've already decided you don't want to do," Brigid said with a laugh. "I don't know how much good that's going to do you, but at least you're ruling out some things."

"Actually," Holly began, after she finished laughing with Brigid. "I'm really leaning towards being a psychologist or having my own business. Like a shop or something," she said.

"Well you know you can run a business fairly well, what with all your experience at the bookstore. But I think starting a business and maintaining it are two different things. Do you know what kind of a store you'd want to start?" Brigid asked.

"Not really," Holly said glumly. "That's probably a pretty vital part, huh?" she asked with a grimace.

"Just a bit," Brigid answered.

"How did Fiona decide she wanted to open a bookstore?" Holly asked.

"Let's grab a smoothie, and I'll tell you how I remember it. By the way, I heard the place over there makes the best smoothies ever. A friend of mine said she drives here just for the peanut butter and banana smoothie. That sounds so good right now. I'm having one, join me?" Brigid asked as she pointed to the smoothie stand a few feet away from them.

"Have you ever seen me turn down food of any kind?" Holly asked. "Of course I'll join you." Actually, all their talking had made them both a little parched and in need of a break. When they got their smoothies, Holly pointed to a bench and they sat down to rest and drink them.

"Let me guess, Fiona probably always wanted to open a bookstore," Holly sighed. "She seems like the type of person who has always known what she wanted to do right from the start."

"Actually, no," Brigid said, surprising Holly. "She really wanted to be a fashion designer."

"Seriously?" Holly asked. "Why didn't she become one?"

"There were a few factors involved. But most of all, Fiona didn't like to play by the rules. You know how she is. You'd think that would be a good thing in the fashion industry, but I guess it wasn't where she went to school. Eventually, she dropped out because she couldn't do it anymore. She said her love for it was just gone," Brigid said sadly.

She still remembered some of the amazing things her sister had sketched and sewn up. Although they'd often been simple, they were always unique.

"That's kind of sad," Holly mumbled. She looked almost defeated and Brigid realized she needed to get to the point. Telling a girl who is trying to decide what to do with her life that people don't achieve their dreams is not what Holly needed to hear.

"Not really. It was when she was at fashion school that she discovered her passion for books. Granted, she probably would have found it eventually, but that's when it came to her, and that's the way it seems to be for most people.

"Finding what your passion is can be a winding road that sometimes doubles back or seems to take you in circles. But if you just keep doing your best and following what makes you happy, you'll get there."

Brigid felt the same could be said for her. Of course, she still loved editing professionally and enjoyed seeing what her clients came up with next, but there was something about the occasional work she did with the sheriff's department that seemed to make her feel younger. As if it breathed life into her when she was able to help solve a case. After all, nobody had ever said you could only have one calling in life.

"I see what you're saying. Stop stressing and go with what feels right," Holly surmised. "Because you never know what life has in store for you."

"Now you're getting it," Brigid said as she nodded. "You'll need to get basic classes out of the way first, and in the meantime, you could take a class in your chosen area to see how you feel about it. I knew a couple of people who swore they were meant for one thing, but once they started studying it, they realized they hated it."

"What did they do?" Holly asked, wide-eyed.

"They just changed their major and moved on. You'd be surprised how often that happens. If I were going to give you one piece of advice, it would be that nothing is set in stone."

"For some strange reason, that does make me feel better," Holly admitted. "There's one college I'm really considering, and they have a lot of different programs," she explained.

"Oh? Where's that?" Brigid asked as she continued to slurp her smoothie.

"Um, Missouri State," Holly said as she looked away nervously.

"I see," Brigid said. "Where is that in Missouri? Springfield, I take it?"

"Yeah," Holly said, nervously biting her lip. "I thought it would be nice to be somewhere where I already knew someone, like my cousins, and that would also get me out of Colorado. But I haven't made my mind up yet. It's just an idea," she said quickly as if she was afraid Brigid might be upset.

"Hey, I don't mind. If you want to go out of state, I'd rather you go where you know some people. I think I'd sleep better," Brigid chuckled. "Besides, after I got to meet your mother's family at your birthday party, I really liked them. They seem to be good people."

"You wouldn't be mad if I did that?" Holly asked, hesitantly.

"Of course not," Brigid said as she put her arm around Holly. "But I still want you to come home sometimes to visit."

"Are you kidding?" Holly asked. "I'll always come back to visit. I mean, I know I don't call you and Linc, 'Mom and Dad,' but you're still family and parents to me. There's no way I could just leave that all behind."

"Then if you're happy, I'm happy," Brigid said as she finished her smoothie. "Now let's get back to shopping. And I'll have to tell my friend that she was right about that smoothie. It's the best I've ever had." She stood up and tossed her empty cup into a nearby trashcan, and cheered loudly when she made it. Holly just laughed and shook her head as she carefully dropped hers in, instead of attempting a long basketball type of shot.

CHAPTER FOUR

Luis Lopez had been working for Jesse long enough to remember what things used to be like back before Jesse had become the big guy that he was now, doing all the illegal and shady stuff. It was all so much simpler before Jesse opened the club and used it as a front for his drug running.

He rolled over in bed and looked at his beautiful wife. *I would do anything to be able to get away from him just for her,* he thought. He wished he had a stable job that didn't put him in jeopardy of being arrested or worse. He drank in every dip and curve of her face in the dappled sunlight that filtered through the window curtain, so thankful that she'd chosen him.

"Hey, baby," she said as she opened her sleepy brown eyes and saw him staring at her. "What's wrong?" She lifted her head and readjusted her pillow before brushing her hair back from her face.

"Nothing," he said softly as he kissed her nose. "Did you sleep well?"

"Always when I'm with you," she said with a smile. She paused and saw the sober look on his face. "Luis, what's wrong?"

"I have a meeting with Jesse today," he said forlornly. He wasn't looking forward to it. Every time he thought about it, he had a sinking feeling in his stomach.

"Oh, baby. I can't wait until you can quit working for him. You deserve more. You're so much better than he is," she said as she leaned over and gave him a loving kiss. "I'll go and make breakfast for us."

She tossed the blankets back and climbed out of bed. He watched her walk out of their bedroom, and he wished for the millionth time that things were different. Yet at the same time, he wondered if he and Marielle would be where they were if Luis hadn't agreed to work for Jesse right from the start.

He climbed out of bed and began collecting his clothes before he headed into the bathroom. Marielle knew that he worked for a bad man, but he'd always made sure she wasn't aware of the part he played. He didn't want her to know just how much bad he'd done in his life, and certainly not the things he'd done since they'd been together. Fear that she would see him differently made him keep all those things a secret. The less she knew, the better.

Turning on the water, Luis knew that before he'd met Marielle, what he'd done hadn't worried him. He could do whatever dirty work Jesse threw his way and not even bat an eye. He'd lost count of how many bones he'd broken and the amount of money he'd collected on Jesse's behalf over the years. Because of it, he and Marielle lived well.

Jesse had definitely rewarded him for his loyalty, but times had changed. Luis wasn't the feisty young man that he used to be. Now he had kids and a family. That changed a man. He couldn't break someone's kneecap and then go home and read his little girl a bedtime story. His heart had softened, and he'd begun to see the world in a gentler light.

When Jesse had called Luis and told him he wanted him to come in so they could talk about Mike Loomis, he'd started to get a burning sensation in his stomach. Unfortunately, it hadn't let up. If anything, it seemed like it was worse.

He knew what was going to be expected of him, and he didn't like it. Things had been getting much more serious with Jesse recently, and whenever he thought someone was a threat to him, he reacted in a way that was going to cause someone some serious problems. From the tone of his messages, Luis didn't think Jesse had good things on his mind.

Lately, when Jesse had sent someone to do his dirty work, he'd become more and more agitated. He also expected his men to go further and further each time. He usually didn't send Luis anymore, since Luis wasn't exactly a young pup. But when Jesse's goons had almost killed the last guy who had crossed Jesse, something seemed to have snapped in the man.

The scariest part was that Jesse acted as if being harsh and brutal was something that should be rewarded. Luis may have been a bit of a tough guy in his day, but he had his limits. He was afraid that things were going too far, and if things got out of hand, he was afraid what that could mean for him and his family.

After he'd showered and grabbed a quick breakfast with his family, Luis was out the door and on his way to the club. He turned the radio up loud when it began to play his favorite song, and he started to sing along, trying to take his mind off of where he was going. Even so, his stomach began to burn again. He dug around in the center console for the antacids he kept there and tossed two in his mouth.

By the time he pulled up to the club, he'd begun to consider if this was the time to ask Jesse to let him out. He could tell him he was considering a different line of work. He and Marielle may have to move, but that wasn't a big deal. He'd do whatever it took to be out from under Jesse's thumb as long as he could live in peace. It's not like other people didn't come and go in Jesse's organization. Once he was at the back door, he paused to roll his neck and relax his shoulders before he entered the building.

There weren't many people in the club at this time of day, and he was thankful for it. Luis hated the thumping music and the crush of human bodies on the dance floor. If he never had to come back here, it would be too soon. Walking quickly and with determination, he approached his boss' office and knocked.

"Come in, Luis," he heard Jesse say.

As he entered, a young woman was tugging her skirt down, looking down bashfully. Meanwhile, Jesse was sitting in his chair, looking pleased with himself. She quickly hurried from the office, shutting the door behind her.

"My man, Luis," Jesse began, "I can always count on you."

"So, what's up?" Luis asked. "You said we needed to talk about Mike Loomis?"

"We do," he said, nodding. "The guy seems to have miraculously shortened his prison sentence, and I'm trying to find out why. But to be honest, I don't want to wait," he explained. "I think we need to move as quickly as possible."

"What do you mean?" Luis asked.

Jesse stood up from his chair and began to pace back and forth. "What I mean is, I think he's a rat. He knows far too much about our operation for me not to be concerned. I think we need to eliminate that particular concern completely."

"I don't know, Jesse, don't you think that's risky?" Luis asked. "If he did roll, how do you know he's not being watched?" This was his worst nightmare coming to life.

"I have guys checking on that right now," he said. "I should hear back pretty soon about his routine and what he's been doing. But I've been thinking about him, and he's still just too much of a risk. Luis, we've built far too much to have it jerked out from under us now."

Luis noticed he was using "us" and "we." That meant he was trying to build Luis up so that he'd be willing to go along with whatever Jesse's crazy notion was. He'd seen his boss use that technique on the other guys before.

"I get that, but if I rough him up and the law traces it back to us, we'll be in trouble," he pointed out.

"Which is why you won't be roughing him up, my friend," Jesse said as he stopped pacing. "I want you to make him disappear, as in completely."

Luis felt the hair on the back of his neck rise. This wasn't good. "Jesse, that's not really my thing," he began.

"I know it's not," Jesse said as he moved over to the window that looked out over the club. "Which is why, if you do this for me, I'll give you what you most desire."

Luis furrowed his brow. What was he talking about? "What do you mean?" he finally asked.

"Look, I know your heart just isn't in all of this anymore," Jesse said as he turned back around. He leaned against the ledge, his gelled black hair shining in the light. A grin played across his lips, a grin that unsettled Luis. "You want to put all of this behind you and spend the rest of your days lounging around with that family of yours, correct?"

"Well, yeah. That would be nice," Luis admitted.

"Do this for me, and I'll make it happen," Jesse said. "You kill Mike Loomis and give me back my peace of mind. In return I'll give you your peace of mind. Fair trade." He crossed his arms, waiting for Luis' response.

"And what if I don't feel comfortable doing that?" Luis asked.

"Oh, I think you will," Jesse said as he stood up and started walking towards Luis. There was a glimmer in his eye that Luis hadn't seen before and it made him nervous. He almost wished he hadn't said that last sentence as Jesse strolled across the floor, a calm but calculated look on his face.

Once he was directly in front of Luis, Jesse spoke again. "Because if you don't, you won't have a family to go home to. I will ensure that someone who is much more capable takes care of them and then takes care of you. Unfortunately, they'll do things to your family that I really don't want to happen. I'd much rather give you a nice nest egg and send you on your way." He was still grinning in that twisted way that made Luis want to shiver.

"I hear you," Luis said showing more bravado than he felt. "It will take a little time. I want to make sure I strike at the right time, so there's no blowback on us."

"I trust your judgment," Jesse said finally. "And I'm glad you see things my way."

Luis nodded. "I'll start planning for it immediately."

"Good, I will too," Jesse said as he returned to his desk. "That's all I needed. I don't want to hear from you until it's done."

Luis nodded before turning to leave. He didn't see that he had much choice. He was going to have to murder Mike Loomis in order to keep his family safe. There was no way he'd let his job hurt the ones he loved.

Plus, once it was over, he'd be free. Luis remembered Mike, and while he didn't have anything personal against the guy, the dude had done his fair share of bad back in the day. *I'm sure he has a couple of people who would like to see him dead,* he rationalized. *There would be no reason for anyone to look at me.*

Although Luis didn't like it, he'd do whatever it took to protect his family.

CHAPTER FIVE

Brigid pulled her car up at her sister's house, ready to go on one of their regular walks. She knew they wouldn't be happening as often once the weather turned, but for now, she cherished the time alone with Fiona.

Sometimes Holly tagged along, and that was fine, but she really liked these alone times with her sister just a tad more. When it was just the two of them, they could talk about anything without fear of upsetting teenage ears. And now that they were adults, it seemed like she and her sister were closer than they'd ever been before.

"Hey," Fiona said as she opened the door before Brigid could even knock. "I'm just getting Aiden in his stroller. Give me a minute." She walked away from the door, leaving it standing open for her sister.

"No problem," Brigid said. "Take your time." She casually walked around her sister's living room as she waited. "You know, Holly hadn't ever heard that you wanted to be a fashion designer," she began.

"Oh?" Fiona said as she finished buckling Aiden in. "Well, I guess she wouldn't have. It's not like I really talk about it anymore," she admitted. "I'm not ashamed of it. It's just a part of who I used to be. Nothing more."

"Do you still do it sometimes?" Brigid asked. "Design, I mean? I remember you used to have notebooks filled with ideas. You'd even steal my markers and colored pencils when yours ran out. That used to make me so mad," Brigid said with a smile.

"Sorry," Fiona said meekly.

"It's too late for that," Brigid said, waving her hand. "You were just doing what you loved, that's all. No harm in that. But do you?"

"I think about it mostly," Fiona admitted. "Especially now that I have Aiden. But yeah, I still have a notebook or two I like to jot ideas in. I just can't help it." She went to the coat rack near the door and grabbed a jacket. "Ready when you are."

Brigid took Aiden's stroller and pushed it over to the door while her sister opened it. Soon they were out in the fresh autumn air. "Why don't you do something with them?" Brigid asked after they'd been walking for a few minutes.

When Fiona looked confused, Brigid continued. "Your drawings. Why don't you make them? You were really good at making clothes in high school. I remember when practically every girl in school wanted you to alter her jeans or shorts. You were destressing them, adding patches and fabric, along with all sorts of other neat things. It was amazing," Brigid reminisced.

"I'm too busy now," Fiona said, blowing it off. "Besides, that was a long time ago. Why are you bringing up that old stuff?" she asked. Others may have thought she was being cranky, but Brigid knew better.

"I was talking with Holly about college the other day. She's unsure what she wants to do, and I was explaining that sometimes our plans take unexpected detours that work out in the end," Brigid summarized.

"Life definitely does that," Fiona scoffed. "If you would have told me back then where I'd end up, I would have told you that you were nuts."

"Me too, and that was my whole point," Brigid said. "But it seems to have worked out in the end."

"We're both doing okay, aren't we?" Fiona said with a satisfied smile.

"That we are," Brigid said. "And you seem happier now. I was really worried about you there for a while. Feel like you've got that postpartum depression dealt with?"

"I think so," Fiona said with a nod as they stopped at a corner for traffic. They waited until it was clear before crossing the street. "I still have days that aren't terrific, but I think that's probably normal. And if I don't work out and eat right, I can sure tell the difference. The doctor took me off my meds, so I must be doing something right."

"Good," Brigid said happily.

"For a while, I thought about hiring someone else for the bookstore," she confessed. "I just wasn't sure I could do it anymore. All I wanted to do was sleep, and I had so much to do, and I'm not even including dealing with the bookstore stuff."

"Why don't you hire someone?" Brigid asked. "It sure would take a little off your plate," she pointed out. Actually, now that she thought about it, Brigid was surprised her sister hadn't done it sooner.

"Yeah, it would," Fiona agreed. "But then what would I do in my free time?" she asked with genuine curiosity. The bookstore had been her life for so long she wasn't sure she could leave it in someone else's hands.

"Sketch some great clothes and maybe even make them?" Brigid suggested. "Or refurbish clothes like you used to do. Some of the stuff you did was brilliant."

Brigid knew she was pushing it, but ever since the conversation with Holly, her mind had been focused on her sister and the fact that she'd given up her dream. Sure, the bookstore was a huge success, but it wasn't where her heart truly was. There was absolutely no reason for her sister not to give it a shot at this point. The bookstore would run just as well if she was off a few extra days.

"I don't know," Fiona said. "It would be quite a stretch."

"Just think about it," Brigid said. "The world is a very different place than it was back then. Today you can practically start your own clothing line online all by yourself. You don't need a fancy college degree or connections to the right people. You have the internet now. Make an online store, run a few ads, and start getting visitors. You just have to stick to it."

"But I love working at the store," Fiona said. "I couldn't ever just not work there. It's like my second home."

"I'm just saying," Brigid said quickly, "that you were so good at what you did. Freeing up time to try it out again isn't a bad idea. Nobody said you can't still work at the bookstore a few days a week if you want. Just step back as much as you feel comfortable. Besides, I think it's a wonderful idea to hire more help. Then you can learn to relax a bit more." She gave Fiona a wink and a nudge.

"I relax," Fiona pouted. But she knew exactly what her sister was talking about. "I may not do it exactly like you do, but I still relax."

"Oh, that reminds me," Brigid began. "Linc wants to turn his house into a B & B."

"Really?" Fiona asked, surprised. "And what did you say?"

"I told him I'd think about it," she said. "But I'm starting to like the idea."

"You'd be awfully tied down," Fiona pointed out. They had to take a break, because Aiden started getting fussy. Fiona gave him a drink and he calmed down.

"I know, but Linc seemed to have a plan for that," Brigid said. "He says we could always find someone to help us out and manage it if we want to go somewhere or if something comes up."

"How does Rich feel about that? After all, he's got the only B & B in town right now," Fiona asked.

"Actually, he's the one who put the idea in Linc's head, if you can believe that. He said he's often completely booked up and would love somewhere else to refer people. So Linc thinks it's a great plan," Brigid sighed.

"And you don't?" Fiona surmised.

"No, I do. I'm just nervous. It's a huge commitment," Brigid began.

"You know what I've learned to do when something has me going in both directions?" Fiona asked. "I try to get some quiet time with my thoughts. The trails up around the ski lodge are great for that. You could take Jett with you. He'd love it," she pointed out.

"And that helps you clear your head?" Brigid asked.

"Sure does. There aren't any distractions up there. I just think of my issue like I'm asking a question to someone and then see what crops up as I walk. Sometimes I've surprised myself," she admitted.

"Thanks, maybe I will," Brigid said. "It's been a long time since I've done something like that. Usually I just clear my head and go with the flow. Maybe it's time I tried something different."

"It couldn't hurt," Fiona said. "You might just have an epiphany."

"I wouldn't go that far," Brigid chuckled.

"No, seriously," Fiona said shaking her head. "Sometimes, when

I'm doing that… never mind," she said quickly. "You'd think I was crazy. Heck, maybe I am." She looked down sadly.

"What?" Brigid asked softly. "You can tell me."

"Well, it might sound strange, but sometimes I swear I can hear our parents answer my question," she muttered.

"Really?" Brigid asked, surprised. "Like what?"

"It's not like I physically hear them, it's more like a thought transmitted in their voice," she explained. "Like I can just hear what they would say. It's hard to explain," Fiona said with a sigh and shook her head. "Forget I said anything."

"No, I think I know what you mean," Brigid continued. "I get that sometimes too. Like if the house is quiet, and I'm doing something, but my mind is elsewhere. I'll have a thought and then something Mom would say just pops into my mind out of nowhere."

"Exactly," Fiona nodded. "Sometimes I'll even wonder where it came from."

"I get it," Brigid nodded. They both walked quietly for some time with the only sound being Aiden blowing raspberries and amusing himself. "Do you really think it's them?" she finally said.

"I like to think it is," Fiona said, her voice thick. "Melanie told me it was. Especially when it comes out of nowhere or there's just a random memory that comes up. She said it's their way of communicating with me. She told me that's actually how she gets information, too. Only for her, there's a bit more, and it comes from all sorts of places."

"That's amazing," Brigid said. "Sometimes I wish I could do that. Talk to spirits, I mean. There's so much I'd like to say. I just can't believe how long they've been gone."

"I know," Fiona said, her eyes getting slightly misty. "I think about how I wish they were here, so they could see Aiden. I'd love to watch Dad count his fingers and toes over and over like he did to every baby he met."

"Oh, that's right," Brigid chuckled. "And with some of them, he would pretend like the baby was missing a toe or something just to freak out the parents." Both of them laughed.

"He loved doing that," Fiona commented. "He was such a goof."

"For sure," Brigid nodded. "But boy did he love Mom."

"Now that's a fact," Fiona said. "It's crazy how after Mom passed, he didn't last much longer."

"Well, five and a half years," Brigid pointed out.

"Still, that's not terribly long," Fiona said. "I was just getting to where I could remember her and not cry when he got sick too. Of course, he didn't give us the full story. She rolled her eyes. "Not that I'm really surprised."

"He didn't want us to worry," Brigid said. "He went the way he wanted. That's what counts."

"Amen," Fiona said. "Now let's stop talking about the past before I ruin my makeup. Come on, let's take a detour for a piece of banana split pie."

"Seriously?"

"Yes. Best ice cream thing I've ever had. I discovered it when I was pregnant. It's just this little hole in the wall diner around the corner. Trust me on this one. I mean who wouldn't like vanilla, strawberry, and chocolate ice cream with fudge sauce on a vanilla crust?"

"Say no more," Brigid said. "I'm salivating. Hurry up."

CHAPTER SIX

Derek Walden had been making good money as the local drug dealer for Cottonwood Springs and the surrounding area. However, he wasn't foolish enough to make it his only source of income. That was a good way to bring attention to yourself that you didn't need or want when you were dealing drugs.

He had a good job at the local RV factory and made it a priority to rarely dip into his own supply, which was something the previous guy hadn't been very good at. It hadn't taken long for Derek to hear all about how terrible Mike Loomis was about using the drugs he was supposed to be selling. Plus, the only job the guy had was at a B & B and that didn't justify some of the money he'd flash around from time to time. No, Mike Loomis hadn't been a very smart guy.

It was time for his lunch break, so Derek collected his things and got ready to go out to his car. He looked forward to lunchtime each day because it meant one thing. Once lunchtime came, he could start drinking. Although he didn't have a big drug problem, his love for alcohol was practically legendary. He clocked out and pushed open the door that led outside, breathing in the fresh air and imagining the burn of the soon-to-be-consumed alcohol at the back of his throat.

Derek had been living just outside of Cottonwood Springs for some time now. He'd rented a house in the country around the time he'd started dealing. That way, there weren't any nosy neighbors to turn him in for the constant flow of traffic coming and going from his house. There was no one around to become suspicious of what he or the people who came to his house were doing. One thing he'd learned long ago was not to trust your neighbors when you were in the drug business. Neighbors had been responsible for the demise of a lot of drug dealers.

It had happened to his cousin Marcus, and he'd be darned if the same thing was going to happen to him. Of course, Marcus was stupid enough to try to cook the drugs right there in town. Derek knew better. That was just a recipe for disaster.

After he climbed into the front seat of his car, he turned the key in the ignition and rolled the windows down. He pulled out the whiskey bottle he had hidden under his seat and took a long pull before reaching for the seat lever and leaning back.

He closed his eyes and let the alcohol begin to work its way through his system. He hadn't really wanted to come into work today, but he didn't have any more time off, and he needed a full paycheck. He had too many bills coming up, and he still needed to get more supply.

A knock on his window pulled him from his peace, causing him to jerk his eyes open. When he turned toward the window, he saw it was Evelyn, one of the ladies who liked to get her supply from him. He couldn't be rude to her if she wanted to give him some money, so he signaled for her to climb in. It wasn't like he could hide from her.

"Hey, Derek, how's it going?" she asked as she climbed inside his car. Her dark hair was pulled back in a pony tail, but there were wispy strands that had escaped from it. She was older and a little heavy, but he still thought she was good-looking.

"Not too bad," Derek said easily as he brought his seat back up to an upright position. "You need a pick-me-up?"

"Maybe later," she said as she looked around. She didn't seem to be paranoid. It was more like she was looking for someone. "I just wanted to see if you'd heard about Mike?"

"Mike?" he asked, confused. "Mike who?"

"Mike Loomis? You know, the guy who used to be the main man for this area if you needed a fix? He's out." she said.

"What do you mean he's out?" he asked, focusing on her. "Like he got out early from prison?" He began to feel irritated.

She nodded. "That's exactly what I'm saying. He's out and he's living in Cottonwood Springs. You think he's planning on setting up shop again?" she asked. Her eyes were wide as if she was trying to act innocent.

He could see she was hopeful, and he reckoned Mike probably used to give her a deal in exchange for certain kinds of favors. Derek wasn't that kind of dealer, and she knew it. Evelyn was probably looking to get her fix from Mike if he was getting back in the game.

"I have no clue," he admitted. "But I'm sure if he does then his stuff would be sub-par compared to mine."

"Your stuff is good, I'll give you that," she agreed. "I just wanted to see if you'd heard he was back. I didn't know if you'd be worried, but I figured you'd probably like to have a heads up."

"Why would I be worried?" Derek asked, becoming indignant. "Who'd want to buy from someone who was sloppy enough to get caught once before? That's like putting a sign in your yard just telling the cops you're a user. Anyone who goes to visit him would have to be an idiot."

Evelyn realized she'd struck a sensitive nerve and started backpedaling. "Hey, man. I didn't say I was going to buy from him. I just wanted to give you a heads up," she said as she held her hands up as if in surrender. She caught sight of one of their co-workers and nodded to him. "I'm going to go see what Shane's up to. I'll catch you later," she said as she opened the door and climbed out.

Derek had been having a fairly good day until his conversation with Evelyn. The whiskey mixed with anger was warming his blood, and he was starting to see red. How dare Mike Loomis come back and think he was going to just pick up where he'd left off. That's not how things worked around here.

No, Derek had worked hard to establish himself. It had taken a lot of time, money, and networking to get to where he was now. There was no way he'd step back and let some guy just walk in and take over. Not without a fight.

Reaching for the whiskey bottle, Derek took another long pull from it, this one longer than before. He needed to calm himself down before he headed back into work. Otherwise, this day could get a lot worse. The only thing on his mind was making sure Mike Loomis knew that he wouldn't be selling around these parts. Not now, not ever. This was his area now. If he wanted to start selling again, Mike would have to relocate.

Unfortunately for Derek, the whiskey did nothing to cool his temper. If anything, it was like throwing gasoline on a fire with the hopes of putting it out. All it did was cause his anger to grow until he was shaking as he sat in his car. The more he thought about the situation, the madder he got.

How dare that guy think after all this time he could just come waltzing back and pick up where he left off? he thought.

The alcohol was causing him to jump to conclusions that he wasn't even sure were correct. It was as if in a blink of an eye, he went from having a normal day to feeling as though he was ready to fight. The only thing he could think about was the fact that he needed to figure out a way to get rid of Mike Loomis. But how?

He pulled out his cell phone and sent a text to one of his friends who had known Mike before he'd been sentenced to prison. Derek had known of Mike, but hadn't known him personally. He didn't have enough background on Mike to know where to look for him. Cottonwood Springs wasn't a big town, but you couldn't just drive into it and start asking people where someone might be.

Plus, he'd heard that the sheriff's department over there was pretty good at keeping an eye on things. He definitely didn't want to draw attention to himself. If anyone could tell him where Mike was now and what he was up to, it was Brit.

Hey man, he texted, *I heard Mike Loomis is out. You wouldn't happen to know where's he hanging out, would you? I'd like to get ahold of him.*

He waited a little bit, not sure if Brit was busy at the moment or not. When he heard the sound signaling he had a message, he felt relieved.

Heard the same. Someone said he was living over at the yellow house old man Foreman rents out, Brit replied.

Is that so? Derek responded. *What's he up to now?* He knew Brit would understand his code.

Not sure, to be honest. Think he's keeping on the low but can't verify. I can find out more info later, Brit responded.

Thanks, man. I appreciate that. Let me know what you find out.

Derek tossed his phone down in frustration. So, Brit didn't know if Mike was back in the game and looking for buyers. Well, maybe the guy hadn't had a chance to yet, but Derek had no intention of letting him. He didn't want to give up even one customer to Loomis. He picked his phone up again and sent a text message to his boss.

Something came up. I'm going to be late coming back from lunch, he sent before starting up his car. He simply couldn't wait to find out. If there was a threat to his main livelihood, he wasn't going to just sit around and let it happen. No, he'd take care of Loomis, one way or another.

He'd be subtle at first, but if he had to, he'd do what was necessary to get the point across. He pulled out of the parking lot and headed toward Cottonwood Springs, not sure how he was going to handle the situation. The town was still fifteen minutes away, so he had a little time to decide.

All he'd probably do for now was determine whether or not Mike lived where Brit had thought he did. If Derek found out that he did, he'd return later and see what kind of traffic was going on. Then he'd probably try spooking the guy.

If Mike was a smart guy, he'd take the hint and look somewhere else to land. And if he didn't? Well, Derek figured he might have to do something a little more drastic. Maybe a little breaking and entering would help or a good old-fashioned beating with a baseball bat.

CHAPTER SEVEN

"Hey Brigid, thanks fer comin' down," Sheriff Davis said as she entered his office. It was a place she'd become fairly familiar with since it was where she and the sheriff met when they needed somewhere to discuss a case.

"I was a little surprised to get a call from you this morning," she said as she took a seat. "It seems as though things have been fairly quiet for a while." Not that she minded having something new to focus on. It had been a while since she'd been assisting the sheriff on a case.

"They pretty much have been," he said, "which I'm happy 'bout. That means I've been doin' a good job, but I got a call from Mike Loomis this mornin'. He thinks someone's harassin' him."

"Mike Loomis?" Brigid asked, more than a little surprised. "I thought he was in prison. It doesn't seem like it's been that long since Lucy was murdered, and it was about that time that he was arrested and sentenced for dealing drugs."

"Yer' right," Sheriff Davis said. "But he was released a l'il while ago fer good behavior. Looks like he tried to keep a low profile when he got out. Ya' know, tryin' to blend in and all of that. He's under the impression that some of his old associates are messin' with him."

"He thinks someone is harassing him?" she asked. "Why would he think that?" Surely people have forgotten about him after all this time.

Sheriff Davis rifled through the papers on his desk in search of his notes. "He's got a few legitimate reasons for thinkin' it," he said. Finally, he found his legal pad and flipped a few pages. "Let's see…," he said as he skimmed through his writing.

"Had a bunch of different things happen. Looks like he had a cat that's gone missin'. Said his garage was ransacked and that people keep ringin' his doorbell, but when he answers it, nobody's there. Ya' know, stuff like that. To be honest, Brigid, ain't so sure he's not on the stuff again." He sighed as he tossed the pad back down on his desk.

"If that's the case, why did you call me in?" she asked. She wasn't sure how she was supposed to help Mike if he was back to his old ways. Seemed like some people just couldn't let old habits die, even when they did nothing but harm the person.

"Well, can't exactly take his report and not at least keep an open mind. After all, he was a big drug runner for these parts. I'm thinkin' maybe someone's tryin' to send him a message," Sheriff Davis speculated.

"These drug guys can get real serious 'bout their territory. Ya' might not think so 'round here, since it's jes' a small town with simple ways, but the truth of the matter is, a lot of these people answer to someone bigger than them and located outta' town. I'd bet when he was dealin' he met up with some serious dudes who don't want him to go straight, but if somethin' goes down, means I didn't do my job."

"I suppose that's possible," Brigid said, "and I can't say that I blame you for looking into it. It's hard telling what he may have been wrapped up in. But I'd bet that it's more likely he's picked up an old habit, and it has him thinking things are happening that aren't. After all, cats go missing. He could also have just misplaced things. And if he's using, the doorbell could be a hallucination happening because of his paranoia."

"That's the way I'm leanin'," he said with a nod. "I'm only human and can't help thinkin' he's up to his old ways, but I can't jes' ignore his concerns until I got a reason to suspect otherwise.

"But here's the thing. I'm in a bit of a bind, Brigid. See, most of my deputies are either on vacation or have enough on their plate as it is. If this is real and not just Mike's imagination, I need someone with a good all-round perceptive on things to look into it.

"I gotta' head out of town for a coupla' days fer a conference. I knew when I agreed to speak at it, I'd probably end up regrettin' it, but I did it anyway. So now I'm havin' to make sure someone keeps an eye on my cases while I ain't here."

He leaned forward as if there was someone else in the room who could overhear what he was saying. "And I ain't sure my deputies would handle Mike's case with the tact that I know ya' would."

His words made Brigid swell with pride. "Why thank you," she said with a slight nod. "I take that as a compliment."

"Meant it as one," he said leaning back. "Here's what I'm gonna' do. I've asked my deputies to jes' drive by on occasion when they're out on patrol. Don't know if they'll actually do it, but I'd like to think they will.

"But here's the problem. Most of 'em were on duty when Mike was around before and they ain't exactly fans of his, if ya' know what I mean. There were a few grumbles when I made the suggestion, but I tol' 'em it's their civic duty. They seemed to straighten up at that. I was hopin' that if yer' out and about and could jes' drive by and have a look…"

"Not a problem," she said. "I can see where they might not be willing to help him. He did put your department through the wringer for quite a while."

"That he did," he said shaking his head. "That man was a burr in my behind fer far too long, but I'm tryin' to put all that behind me. If he's keepin' his nose clean, he don't need any extra trouble which might push him back to the other side of the law. If he's straightenin' up, I don't wanna' be a link in the chain that pulls him back to that side."

"I completely understand. I wouldn't want to either," Brigid agreed. "So, you're speaking at a conference?"

"Well, yeah," he said bashfully. "To be honest, I kinda' got roped into it." It was the first time Brigid had ever seen the sheriff look sheepish. She knew there was far more to this story than he was letting on.

"Oh?" she said innocently. "How's that?"

"I may have a friend in law enforcement that let slip 'bout our little bust of those guys doin' the human traffickin'. She passed it on to someone in charge of organizin' the convention, and they asked me to speak 'bout how it all came to pass. Course I'll be sure to credit ya' for all yer' work. I ain't a glory hog," he said as he looked away. Brigid picked up on what he'd said though.

"She?"

"Oh, well, yeah," he said turning red.

"Sounds like she's got some serious sway over you, Sheriff Davis. Have you two gone out?"

"Nah," he said. "Ain't got time fer things like that."

"Sometimes you have to make time," Brigid pointed out. "If she's special, you should."

"Jes' don't know how to approach the whole thing," he admitted. "Ain't never been what ya' might call a ladies man."

"Sounds like she doesn't care," Brigid pointed out. "Maybe while you're at this conference you could ask her out to dinner. That is, if she's going?"

"She is," he said with a nod. "Maybe yer 'right. Been a long time, though."

"Make sure you take something besides your uniform to wear," Brigid pointed out.

"Ah. Brigid, even I know that," he chuckled.

"Hey, I'm just trying to help," she said with a laugh. "Lord knows I haven't seen you in anything but your uniform for quite some time now."

"Yeah. Maybe it's time to let my hair down a l'il' bit," he sighed.

"Well, enjoy yourself while you're out of town, and I'll handle Mike Loomis while you're away," Brigid promised. "Let me know if I need to do anything else."

"Will do," he said as she stood up. "See ya' when I get back."

*****

"Do you really think someone's bothering him?" Linc asked after Brigid had returned home and explained why Sheriff Davis had called her in.

"Honestly, it's hard to say. On one hand, it's very possible. I mean, he could have made some serious enemies when he was dealing. Actually, he probably did. On the other hand, he could have gone back to drugs and paranoia is setting in," she explained as she started to gather the ingredients for cooking some chicken breasts in the slow cooker. She'd been looking forward to trying this recipe along with the mushroom caps in red wine. Both had sounded delicious.

"I hope that's not the case," Linc sighed. "I'd like to think that drugs aren't as much of a problem around here as they once were."

"I think drugs will always be a problem. Especially when we live in a world where it's so easy to get them and things are so tough for so many people. In the short time I've been working with the sheriff's department, I've seen a lot of people who just want to escape their day-to-day reality and drugs are how they do it.

"It seems like most of the time their family, usually their parents, did the same thing. It's heartbreaking," Brigid said. She felt terrible for those people. She knew that some of them were too far down the road to ever come back, but the others? She felt that the others just needed someone to care about them.

"Well, I think you're amazing," Linc said as he gave her a kiss on the cheek.

"Two things," Brigid said as she finished adding the rest of the ingredients and then put the lid on the slow cooker. "First of all, I know you're going to love this chicken and dumplings recipe, along with the mushroom caps. Secondly, I've been thinking about the B & B idea, and I'm on board."

"Really?" he asked. "What made you decide?"

"Well, I remembered that great B & B we went to for our honeymoon in San Antonio. I thought about the owner and his wife, who was deceased, and how they'd planned to grow old together running it. It made me think that I'd like to grow old with you doing that." She sashayed up to Linc with a sly grin. "Among other things."

"Now you're talking," he said as he pulled her close. He gave her a long, deep kiss that made her forget where she was for a brief moment. "Thank you," he said when they finally pulled apart.

"No, thank you," she said. "Now, we still have a little time before Holly comes home and dinner's ready. What would you like to do?"

"I can think of a few things," he said as he tugged on her hand, telling Jett and Lucky to stay. He led her through the house to the bedroom and closed the door.

CHAPTER EIGHT

Jeremy Duggins felt as though his stomach had hit the ground when he'd heard that Mike Loomis had gotten out of prison early. Like it had seriously dropped from its place beneath his lungs and landed at his feet with a thud. Truthfully, he'd been a little nervous after Mike had been arrested. It was common knowledge that when people were arrested, they often gave information to law enforcement personnel in exchange for a lesser sentence.

Since there was no way to predict who would turn on who in that kind of a situation, Jeremy had been worried. He'd even gone so far as to get rid of the stash of drugs he had in his possession as quickly as possible, because he was sure he'd end up getting raided.

Every evening as he sat in his living room, he'd waited for the police to come banging on his door. But as time passed, he'd decided that nobody was going to come for him. That was when he'd started to relax and gotten back to working his connections. It looked like Mike Loomis must be one of those guys who didn't rat out anybody and everybody as soon as the heat was on them.

Jeremy knew Mike through a mutual friend. They'd met at a party and realized that they could help each other out. Since each of them had their own separate suppliers, they'd figured out that when one of them was low on supplies, often the other wasn't. It was kind of a "you scratch my back and I'll scratch yours" situation. It had worked out well for both of them and a mutual trust had developed.

Jeremy would never have guessed that the next time he'd hear about Mike was while he was standing in line at a hamburger fast food restaurant. He'd been busy deciding what he'd order when he'd heard the two officers standing in front of him start talking about Mike.

It was even more of a coincidence, since he didn't live in Cottonwood Springs. He happened to be passing through and decided to stop and get something to eat. Maybe it was luck, or maybe it was the good Lord looking out for him that day. He wasn't sure, and it didn't really matter. All he cared about was the fact that he'd gotten the facts straight from the source. You couldn't get more reliable information than from the sheriff's department.

As a black man in a predominantly white town, Jeremy's senses were always heightened. Not that he'd ever had trouble in the area, but he couldn't help but notice how the officers watched him as he went by. That was exactly why he'd been paying attention to them in the first place. He tried to fly below the radar, but you couldn't do that if you didn't pay attention to the radar itself.

"Did you hear that the guy who was busted for dealing a while back is out of prison?" the first one had said. Jeremy knew a lot of people who had gone to prison, so his ears had perked up. Was he talking about someone Jeremy knew?

Being in this line of work was hazardous to your freedom, but it sure did pay well. Jeremy didn't do drugs. He only sold them, and only to adults. He had his principles and there was no way he'd ever sell to a kid. Adults had their own problems to worry about. If they wanted to get high to deal with them, so be it. It wasn't his place to judge how they spent their time and money.

"No, who? Someone local?" the other officer asked.

"Mike something," the first one said, trying to remember his last name. "Lewis, Loamquist, um…"

"Loomis?" the second asked with a chuckle.

"Yeah, that's it," the first one said. "Doesn't really seem like it's been that long since he was sent up, does it?"

"No, it doesn't," the other one said. "Maybe he made a deal or something."

That's when Jeremy had noticed he was next in line and needed to order. It didn't matter, he'd heard everything he needed to know. Mike Loomis was out, and he was apparently out because of an early release. It could have been for good behavior or something like that, but what if it wasn't? What if Mike getting released was the beginning of the end for people like Jeremy?

It wasn't unknown for a convict to be released on the stipulation that they help bring others in. Jeremey wasn't an idiot, he watched TV and read stuff online. That day he'd gone home and seriously thought about whether he should find another line of work. But when he looked at his expenses, he knew that wasn't possible. Besides, he was good at what he did. He couldn't quit every time he got a little spooked. If he did, he'd have quit a long time ago.

So now he was sitting in his car just down the street from Mike Loomis' house. With the radio on low, he was passing the time playing a game on his phone. He'd done some searching online and found out where Mike was living. Jeremy wanted to make sure he had the right place before he started to send his message.

He thought he'd start off subtle, in hopes his old friend would get the point. He really didn't want to get forceful. But he had to stake the place out before he did anything and make sure he was messing with the right person. If he sent a message to the wrong person, it would probably involve law enforcement, law enforcement which might be pointed in his direction.

While he was sitting in his car slowly passing the time, he noticed an official looking car pull up in Mike's driveway and a stuffy looking white guy climbing out of the driver's seat. If the guy was trying to blend in, he wasn't doing a very good job of it. Jeremy could tell he was some sort of an official guy.

He could be anything from an undercover detective working with Mike or just a parole officer checking in on him. He couldn't tell for certain. Whatever, Jeremy didn't want to be noticed by whoever it was, and if Mike hadn't mentioned Jeremy's name to the man, there was certainly no need to remind him to. It had been a while since he'd spoken to Mike, even before he was busted, and there was always the chance Mike had forgotten about him and their dealings.

The guy strolled up the walk to the house and knocked on the front door. Although it hadn't taken long for the door to open, try as he might, Jeremy couldn't see who answered it. He sighed and leaned back in his seat, continuing to play the game on his phone. Hopefully, when the stuffy guy came back out, he'd be able to see if it was Mike.

He was still staring at the closed door when his phone began to ring and startled him. He hurried to answer it before anyone noticed. It wasn't exactly low profile if people in the neighborhood began staring at you.

"What's up?" he said, answering it.

"Hey, man. I'm wondering if I can meet up with you?" He recognized the voice of one of his regulars. "I'm running low and some people are coming over. You got anything?"

"Sure, sure," Jeremy said as he relaxed. "I'm not in town right now though. I'm over in Cottonwood Springs. Can you wait a little while?"

"Yeah, I guess. Just had a rough couple of weeks. No matter how hard I try to manage without it, I just can't do it, you know? I gotta' have it," he explained.

"I hear you," Jeremy sighed. "Just let me wrap up what I'm doing, and I'll head that way. It won't take me but a few more minutes, and then I'll be on the road. Meet you at the regular place in say, twenty-five minutes?" He started readjusting his seat, so he'd be ready to drive.

"Yeah, that works. Thanks, brother, I appreciate it," the man said before hanging up. Jeremy shook his head. He hated it when guys called each other "brother" or "bro." For some reason, it irritated him more when a white guy did it to him. But he knew the guy didn't really mean anything by it, so he shook it off and sighed.

Jeremy looked at what he believed to be Mike's house once again before setting his phone down in the seat beside him. It looked like he'd have to try again some other time. He started his car, put it in gear, and began pulling out of the spot along the street where he'd parked.

He slowly headed down the street getting closer to the house he'd been watching. He saw the front door open, and the stuffy looking man stepped out and began walking to his car while the other person stood in the doorway. As Jeremy passed by the house, he locked eyes with Mike Loomis.

Mike was heavier than he'd been before and not as pale. Jeremy could tell he was off the dope, which was a good thing. Even with the brief glance he had of Mike, it was plain to see that he was much healthier than the last time he'd seen him.

Jeremy had seen that stuff take over people's lives too many times. It chewed them up and spit them out, leaving nothing behind. He never could understand why people would choose meth. It was made from nasty stuff and turned people into something that wasn't human, but to each their own. It was good to see someone get clean and sober.

Mike nodded to Jeremy as he drove by, acknowledging that he'd seen him. Adrenaline shot through Jeremy's veins. Did he just royally screw up? Had he put himself back on Mike's radar? Only time would tell.

But if Mike did have something going on, it was time to send him a message. Something that suggested Mike find somewhere else to land or things might get ugly. Jeremy didn't want to hurt the guy, but he would if he had to. This was business, and friendship never gets in the way of business.

CHAPTER NINE

Brigid, Holly, and Linc had dug out Brigid's old croquet set and set it up in the back yard. Together, with Jett and Lucky playing nearby, they'd started a game. Brigid couldn't believe how long it had been since she'd played, but she had no trouble picking it back up.

Linc had played before, but Holly hadn't, so they gave her a quick rundown of the rules. The three of them were soon laughing and having a good time, not taking the game too seriously, but still trying their best to beat the others.

The sound of Brigid's cell phone ringing on the nearby table interrupted their fun. Hurrying over to where she'd set it down, she answered it, breathlessly. "Hello?"

"Hey, Brigid, it's Davis," Sheriff Davis said.

"Hi, what's up?" she asked as she walked around the side of the house so she could hear him better. The cell reception wasn't always reliable in the back yard.

"Sorry to bug ya', but I need ya' to go talk to Mike Loomis. He called me all in a panic, sayin' he's got proof that someone is messin' with him. He was ravin' about locked doors and pictures, but I couldn't fully understand him. Think ya' could pop over there and see what's up with him? Hopefully, it won't take too much of yer' time," he said with a sigh.

"Sure, just let me change into something a little more professional," she said easily. "It won't take me more than five minutes until I'm on my way."

"I sure appreciate ya', Brigid. Thanks so much. Let me know what ya' find out, ya' hear?" he asked and she knew he meant it. Over their time working together, she and Sheriff Corey Davis had created a very unique friendship. It was absolutely platonic, but loving in its own way.

"Will do," she said before hanging up.

Brigid changed out of her tank top and shorts, pulled her red hair back, and headed out the door. She promised Linc and Holly she'd wouldn't be gone long, and that she'd beat them in the next game when she came back. They nodded and continued to play as she rushed to her car after giving them each a hug. Before long she was pulling up in front of Mike Loomis' home and climbing out of her car.

Mike came rushing out of his house, and then stopped, clearly surprised. "Hey, where are the sheriff's deputies?" he asked. It was apparent he was surprised to see Brigid.

"Nice to see you too," Brigid said. "Sheriff Davis sent me. I work with the sheriff's department. I assure you that I can take care of whatever's going on." She tried not to let the doubtful look he shot her phase her. He looked around, clearly nervous. His eyes seemed to be looking out for any threats that might be nearby. She could tell from the way he was acting that he was certain he was being watched.

"All right," he finally said. "Come on in."

She followed him into his house and was surprised to see that it was neat and tidy. There wasn't much to it, and it looked a bit like a young person's house who was just starting out, but maybe that's kind of how he was now. Getting a fresh start.

There was an older looking, but clean, couch along the wall with a scarred wooden coffee table in front of it. The white walls were devoid of any kind of decorative attempts. A small recliner sat facing an older tube-style television set.

He closed the door and stood nervously next to it, looking towards the adjoining room. Brigid turned to face him, assessing his appearance. He didn't look like a man strung out on drugs. Instead, he seemed to be someone who was just very stressed. "Sheriff Davis told me you have proof someone is harassing you. Can you tell me about it?" she asked gently.

"I do," he said, nodding. "The photos are on my kitchen table. I didn't want to touch them, just in case," he said.

"Please show me," she instructed. If he did have proof, she needed to see it for herself.

He led her through a wide archway to the kitchen and pointed to a small wooden table. There were a handful of photos scattered across the table. Each one was of Mike in various places around town. On one he was outside the grocery store, in another, outside in his yard. She was unable to tell the location of most of them. They were too close up with blurry backgrounds.

"Where did these come from?" she asked.

"When I woke up this morning, they were there on the table," he explained. "And my doors were still locked. I have no clue how whoever did it got in." His hands were shaking, even though he sounded calm.

"Okay, just relax and take a breath," Brigid said, trying to soothe him. "I'll get someone over here to look for fingerprints."

She pulled out her phone and sent a message to Sheriff Davis that they needed an officer sent to Mike's home to collect possible fingerprints. He responded quickly and assured her he'd have one sent right away.

When she'd finished with Sheriff Davis, Mike answered her question. "I'm not sure," he said as he stared at the photos.

"Let's go back in the front room," Brigid said gently as she guided him away from the offending pictures. They obviously were unsettling to him, and she couldn't blame him. After all, knowing that someone had been watching you without your knowledge, and then was able to break into your home while you were asleep, would upset even the calmest of people.

When they were sitting down, she said, "Who do you think might have done this?" She pulled her pen and notebook from her bag and waited for him to answer.

"Well, my first guess would probably be the guy I used to work for. He's got a lot of people under him, so I can't imagine he'd be the one to get his hands dirty."

"What's his name?" Brigid asked.

"Man, I don't know if I should tell you," Mike began. "I mean, I'm no snitch."

"If you don't tell me and they keep it up, you could have even more problems on your hands, and we won't be able to stop them. If you won't tell me, I can't even begin to help you," she pointed out.

Mike was quiet for a few moments while he seemed to internally debate the wisdom of what she was saying. He knew Brigid was right, but it went against everything he'd always stood for. What if they weren't the ones bothering him and he'd given her their name? He'd be turning them over for nothing. If they weren't the ones who'd been harassing him, they sure would be after that. Eventually, he realized there was just no way around it. Not if he wanted to keep breathing.

"Jesse Stanford. He owns a club in Denver. Can't remember the name of it. He's got a lot of flunkies that do his bidding, but his enforcer was always Luis Lopez," he sighed.

"Okay, anyone else?" she asked as she made some notes.

"Well, I wouldn't have thought it earlier, but I saw an old acquaintance the other day. He was driving by my house and staring at it. May be something, may be nothing," he shrugged. "His name is Jeremy Duggins."

"Is he from around here?" Brigid asked.

"I think he's somewhere fairly local, but we never talked about it. He's a black man, so that might help, since there aren't that many around here."

At first Brigid thought that seemed a little racist, but then she realized Mike was just stating a fact. She wrote his name down and then asked, "Why do you think he's a possibility?"

"Jeremy used to sell too," he explained. "He might not be in the game anymore. I just don't know. I'd forgotten about him until I saw him drive by, and he didn't look happy to see me." He shrugged. "Like I said, could be something, could be nothing."

"Is that everyone?" Brigid asked.

Mike seemed to debate for a moment. "Well...," he finally said. "There is one other possibility I can think of, but keep in mind it's just from things I've heard."

"Okay," Brigid said. "Who is it, and what have you heard?"

"This guy, Derek Walden, kind of replaced me as the drug guy when I went away. I hear he's fairly territorial and that he knows I'm back in town. This is all just hearsay, one person passing something along that they heard from somebody else, but usually that's the way it is. If he thinks I'm trying to go back to my old ways, he may feel threatened," he said with a shrug.

"Yes, I can see where he would," she said, nodding. "Okay, is that everyone?"

"That's all I can think of right now," he said. A knock on the door made him jump.

"That should be the officer Sheriff Davis sent to look for fingerprints," she said. "It's okay." She almost felt sorry for him. He did seem clean and sober, although she was sure the situation he was in wasn't good for him staying that way. She watched his hands shake as he looked out the window and confirmed it was an officer.

She walked over to the door, met the officer, and showed him the photos. He assured her he'd check around to see what else he could check for prints.

"Mike, if I were you, I'd stay somewhere else for now," she suggested. "I don't think it's safe for you to be here."

He shook his head emphatically. "I can't afford to do that," he said. "Being an ex con, I don't exactly make big bucks. Plus, that would just show weakness on my part. I know how these people work. If I leave, they'll think they're getting to me."

"But they are," she pointed out. "No need to be a hero about it."

"Trust me, I'm not a hero," he scoffed. "But I'm not going to let them push me from my home, either. I didn't talk, well, until now. I didn't do anything wrong. I'll be darned if I'm going to run away," he said in a determined voice.

"It's your choice," she said simply. "I'll tell the sheriff we want a few more patrols in the area. I'll look into the people you told me about. That way, their suspicion won't be aroused. Maybe I'll be able to fly under their radar."

"You don't know these guys," he said nervously. "They aren't going to like getting attention from anyone. They'll see you as a threat and won't hesitate to silence you," he warned.

"Then I guess it's a good thing I've done my training. I don't spook easily, Mike. I can take care of myself," she assured him.

"All right, well, good luck," he said.

She nodded as she stood up and walked out the door to her car.

CHAPTER TEN

Later that afternoon, Brigid loaded Jett in the car and drove out to the ski resort. In the off season there were trails you could hike on for a little fresh air and exercise. Earlier, when she'd been back home with Linc and Holly, she'd been thinking about the suggestion her sister had made. Taking a walk in order to find some answers seemed like a good way to spend some time. She needed to clear her mind of everything that had been pulling at her, first one way and then the other.

Between Linc wanting to open a B & B, work, worries about her sister, and this new stuff with Mike Loomis, she didn't know what she should focus on. She thought a chance to clear her mind and let go of things for an hour might be exactly what she needed. If nothing else, a little fresh air and exercise couldn't hurt her.

She pulled up to the lodge, unloaded Jett, and clipped his leash to his collar. His nose lifted into the air scenting new smells, and he seemed to smile as his tongue hung out of his mouth. Jett was always eager to go new places and smell new things. Although she'd brought him to the ski resort before, it had been a long time since they'd been there to just take a walk.

"Do you need this as much as I do, big guy?" she asked as she ruffled his dark fur. He looked up at her with his bright, friendly eyes as if to say, *Definitely.* "It's been a while since it was just you and me, huh?"

It was crazy to think that Jett was actually the first member of this new family of hers. When she'd bought the house and the previous owners couldn't take him to their new condo, she'd leaped at the chance to take him. She'd always dreamed of having a dog, but her ex wouldn't allow it. Now, she couldn't imagine what life would be like without Jett. In her mind, Jett was the kind of dog people referred to when they said dogs are man's best friend. He was the epitome of loyal.

Brigid looked for the sign that pointed out the trails at the edge of the parking lot and followed them until she found the trailhead tucked among some evergreens. There was one main trail that was considered the "Backbone" with lots of smaller, winding trails that broke away from it, only to eventually merge back with the main one. Brigid's plan was to just follow her intuition and see where it took her.

She hadn't done much hiking on these trails. To her recollection, the last time she'd been out here, there had only been the main trail. Now, with so many others to explore, she didn't know where to start.

"I'm so glad we decided to do this," Brigid said to Jett as they started down the gravel path. She inhaled a deep, cleansing breath. "I really think I needed to just put everything down for a little bit, let my brain rest, and reconnect with nature."

Birds were flitting around in the trees and a few puffy white clouds were slowly sliding across the vast blue sky. Jett seemed to be listening as he trotted beside her, so she continued talking.

"You know all the stuff I'm talking about. I can't believe someone actually broke into Mike Loomis' house and left those pictures. Talk about creepy. I told Sheriff Davis about it, but I have a strange feeling, and it's not a good one. He didn't want me to do anything quite yet and was having his deputies search for clues, but still. You know sitting back and waiting isn't exactly my strong suit."

She chuckled to herself and smiled. "But there's only so much we can do at this point. It's not like we have much to go on to figure out who did it. That's a pretty spooky message though, and I can't believe Mike won't relocate and go stay somewhere else. I sure would. He's made of stronger stuff than I am, that's for sure.

"But in other news, I'm so glad Fiona is doing better," she went on. "You know, she admitted feeling as though Aiden would be better off without her? I couldn't believe it when she said that. To think that my sister, who had longed for a baby of her own for so long, could actually have thoughts like that just goes to show how powerful postpartum depression can be," Brigid said, sighing.

"The fact that it was able to change her thoughts like that is just mind-blowing to me. I sure feel for all those women who have struggled with it. I wish I could give each of them a hug and let them know just how normal it is to feel like that and that there are people out there who care."

She lapsed into silence for a while as her thoughts took over. The only sounds were the birds singing, the crunch of the dirt on the trail, and Jett's panting. A slight breeze picked up and lifted her hair as it rustled the trees around them. Since no one was around, she leaned over and unhooked Jett's leash. She trusted him to stick by her side, and this way they both could move a little more freely.

"I wish there was more understanding about postpartum depression. Maybe it's just a matter of people becoming better educated and informed. Fiona said her doctor had mentioned a possibility of postpartum when she was pregnant, but didn't really elaborate beyond that. Maybe if there wasn't so much of a stigma around it, women could get the help they need and not suffer in silence wondering what's wrong with them."

As they approached a split in the trail, Brigid paused for a moment to decide which trail she wanted to take. She hesitated for a moment and then took the smaller trail and started down its path. There were a lot more trees down this path, and she couldn't help but stare up at their majestic beauty.

She stumbled over a rock, but still couldn't manage to take her eyes away from their swaying branches. Jett bumped her gently and gave her a little chuffing sound as if to tell her she should be more careful.

"Sorry, Jett. I can't help it," she explained. Her eyes looked down at the ground long enough to see the general direction of the trail before she started looking up again. "I love to stare at the light shining through the branches. It's like little fingers of heaven reaching though them," she sighed. "I know it's just light, but it seems so magical."

Walking along, she was grateful Fiona had suggested that she come up here to clear her mind. It was certainly something she should probably do more often, especially in the warmer months. With so many little trails and things to see, she couldn't imagine it would ever get boring. She even considered bringing Linc or Holly along sometime. They'd probably enjoy the walk as much as she was.

A strange sound pulled her from her reverie. There was a lot of rustling of leaves on the forest floor and then a deep growl that made Brigid stop in her tracks. It was a soft but deep sound that sent a shiver through her body. The beauty of the trees was now forgotten as she stared down at Jett who was blocking the path as he continued to growl. She couldn't believe such a terrifying sound could come from such a big, cuddly dog.

"I've never heard you do that, Jett. What's gotten into you?" she asked as she shook her head and started to go around him. He was making her nervous, but she thought if she ignored him, he'd come around. As she began to step around him, Jett bumped into her and blocked her again. "Jett, what are you doing?" she asked surprised as she stumbled slightly from his gentle nudge.

He was a big dog, so his nudge was enough to push her back a step or two. The hair on his back was standing up now, and she was thoroughly confused as to what was going on. She looked at the area where he seemed to be staring, but she didn't see anything but grass, dirt, leaves, and a few sticks. Certainly nothing out of the ordinary which would cause him behave like he was. "What is it, Jett? What do you see?"

Jett barked sharply as a large snake she hadn't noticed uncoiled from the pile of leaves it had been camouflaged by that was only two feet from the edge of the trail and slithered away. Fear shot through her as she took in its long triangular shaped head and strange pattern along its back.

"Rattlesnake," she shouted at Jett as she grabbed his collar to restrain him. Stunned, Brigid simply stared at the place where the snake had disappeared into the underbrush. She'd stared right at the spot where it was hiding and hadn't seen it because it was so well camouflaged.

"Holy cow," she finally said as she slowly began to come back to her senses. Once she'd seen the snake move it was as if her entire body had locked up. She realized she'd been holding her breath, and she started to breathe again.

It suddenly hit her that if Jett hadn't been there to warn her, she could have been in serious trouble. "Thank you so much, Jett," she said as she released her grip on his collar and leaned over to scratch his ears. "You just saved me. You're such a good boy."

All the possibilities of what could have happened rushed through her mind, and she was incredibly grateful that she'd brought Jett with her. How close had she been to not bringing him? And hadn't she actually told him no before finally giving in to those big, soulful eyes?

The whole thing made her realize that because she wasn't paying attention to what she was doing, things could have gone badly. She very easily could have provoked the snake and been bitten. Granted, Linc and Holly knew where she was, but they wouldn't begin to worry about her for a few hours, and by then it might have been too late.

She knew cell service could be spotty in the mountains, and even if she'd been able to call an ambulance, they still would have had to search for her. This walk could have gone very differently, but thanks to one loyal dog, she was still healthy and safe.

"I think I owe someone a cheeseburger and maybe even an ice cream. What do you say?" she said as she mentally vowed to pay much more attention to where her feet were going. Jett seemed to smile as he trotted ahead of her. Her mind continued to think about other things, but now she was careful about where she stepped. That was one mistake she wouldn't make again.

Walking alone in the wilderness wasn't something to be taken lightly. She realized how foolish she'd been to have her head in the clouds out here.

Just like life, she thought, *you have to pay attention to what you're doing and the path you're on. You can't just walk along with your head in the clouds, trusting that your next step is going to be a safe one.*

You have to think it through and pay attention, because you never know when there may be something dangerous hiding in the brush, ready to strike. And that danger could be anything. It didn't have to be something horrific. After all, if you simply floated through life, never taking care of yourself or your things, life could end up biting you.

Perhaps what happened was a sign, she continued to think. *Maybe I should trust Linc a little more.* She admitted to herself that she was still worried about the idea of running a B & B. Sure, she'd told Linc she'd go along with it and she'd meant it, but that didn't mean that somewhere deep inside she wasn't still wondering if it was a mistake.

This experience told her that she might be focused on the wrong thing. Linc told her he'd take care of it, so maybe she should just take his word for it. After all, she trusted him completely, so why not trust him to handle it? She sighed as she realized that the entire time she'd been worrying about it, it really hadn't been her problem to worry about.

Linc trusted her when it came to working with the sheriff's department and her editing job. He didn't try to pick and choose or tell her what she could or couldn't do. If this was what he wanted, she should stand behind him completely. She knew there would probably be some hiccups along the way, but that's when he'd need her the most.

Brigid came to the conclusion that she needed to stand by him and remind him it would all work out in the end. That was her job as his spouse. To support him, be by his side and help him when he needed it. Linc didn't need her to worry for him. He needed her to see the possibilities, especially if he started to worry and get stressed.

She made her way back to the main trail and began walking a little faster. Feeling her heart pumping and her limbs moving was exhilarating. She realized she had a terrible habit of worrying about things that were too far in the future to do anything about. She made a promise to herself that she wouldn't get ahead of herself.

She'd done what she could for Mike Loomis at the moment. Everything was in someone else's hands at this point, so why fret about it? Linc was in control of putting together the B & B, so that wasn't her problem now either. And Holly? She had her own choices to make. Actually, so did Fiona. Sure, she'd be there with advice and an ear to listen to both of them, but none of the things she'd been thinking about were in her control.

Just breathe, Brigid, she heard a voice saying in her mind. And that's what she did. She took a deep cleansing breath and allowed all of her worries and concerns to simply fall away. Instead, she began to think about all the things that she could concentrate on now that she was letting everyone else worry about their own stuff. There was a novel that needed her editing attention when she got back home, and maybe a few loads of laundry. But for now, she was completely free to worry about nothing and that was an amazing feeling.

"Where do you think we should go to get a burger, Jett?" she asked as they began to loop back around to where she'd parked. "Obviously you can't go inside," she began.

"Woof," he barked, as if to answer.

71

"I know, you're a good boy, and you should be able to go in. I agree that it isn't fair, but there could be people in there that are allergic to dogs and, well, you aren't exactly small enough for me to sneak you in somewhere." Mentally running through the places she could take him, she finally thought of the perfect place.

"I know where we can go. The old drive-in place where they bring your food to the car," she finally said. "How does that sound?"

Jett trotted along as if he was trying to hurry ahead of her to get to the car and she laughed. "In a hurry, huh?" Alright, we'll cut this walk short." Brigid shook her head and smiled. She figured he was eager to cash in and claim his reward.

CHAPTER ELEVEN

"What have you found out?" Brigid asked after she answered a call from Sheriff Davis. She'd been doing housework and welcomed the distraction.

"Not much I'm afraid," he sighed into the phone. "Whoever did it was purty meticulous. The pictures were printed from home and there weren't no fingerprints to tell us who it was. We're still goin' over some prints found at his house, but since they were mixed in with a few others, don't expect to get much from them."

"Well, it was worth a shot," she said glumly. "I tried to convince Mike to relocate, but he seemed pretty determined to stay put."

"Yeah," he sighed. "Well, at least we know it weren't just his imagination. Think we can safely say that it's not all in his head. Looks like someone is messin' with him. I need to look at the roster and see which deputy of mine might be available to watch him.

"I'm thinkin' the best plan at this point in time, since he won't relocate, is to let him stay put and watch him. See if we can get eyes on whoever is botherin' him. I don't think they're gonna' stop with the pictures."

"I don't think so either," Brigid said, shaking her head. She was walking through the empty house, collecting dirty clothes to throw in the laundry. "Seems to me that it's escalating."

"Yep," Sheriff Davis agreed. "Let's hope their next move will be enough fer us to find out who's doin' it and get this taken care of fairly quickly. Never a good thing when people are sendin' messages like them photos. They want Mike to know they're watchin' him."

"I agree," she said as she tossed an armload of clothes in the washer. "And if they were trying to spook him to get him to leave and he doesn't…" She let her sentence hang in the air.

"They're gonna' find more creative ways to get their point across," Sheriff Davis finished. "Go talk to Mike and let him know I'm gonna' be puttin' someone on him. Might take me forty-five minutes or so to send someone out, but I'm on it. If ya' could stay with him until I let ya' know there's someone posted outside of his house, I'd appreciate it. Make sure ya' got your weapon on ya', just in case."

"Will do," she said as she started the washer. "I'm leaving now." She ended the call with the sheriff and pulled on the holster Linc had gotten her for her gun. Since it was cooler out today, she could wear it under her jacket, and no one would be any the wiser. She got her jacket and purse, and in minutes was out the door.

It didn't take long to get across town and pull up in front of Mike's quaint little house. She was sure he'd be relieved to know he was going to have someone guarding him at a distance. Again, Brigid thought he was crazy for staying by himself at home. She wasn't sure she'd be able to do the same if she was in his situation. She knew she wouldn't be able to sleep.

As Brigid was walking up the sidewalk to Mike's house, she was somewhat surprised he hadn't come out to greet her. After all, he had to be even more observant now. When she got to the front door and noticed it was partially open, she became concerned.

"Mike?" she called as she knocked on the door. "Mike, it's Brigid." She paused to listen for any sounds of movement from within the house, but there were none. A sinking feeling settled into her stomach. She knocked once more, harder this time, before she unholstered her gun. Cautiously, she pushed the door to the fully open position and crept inside. She saw a knife and a Buddha statue, both on the floor. It didn't look like Mike had inadvertently knocked the statue over. Something had happened, and it was probably bad.

Brigid considered calling out, but she was worried Mike's attacker, if there was one, could still be in the house. She crept to the archway that led to the kitchen and peeked around the corner. She noticed the back door was open as well, but the glass outer door was shut.

Kitchen cabinet drawers were open as if someone had been searching for something. Vegetables were strewn along the counter, as if Mike had been in the middle of making a salad. Brigid knew it would be important to check the drawers, but first she wanted to make sure no one was in the house. She was glad the house wasn't big. Even though she'd learned how to properly search a house in one of her law enforcement courses, she didn't want to have to check a large one on her own.

Silently, she made her way around the side of the living room to the two nearby doors. The first one opened to a tiny bathroom with a shower stall and a small sink in it. She flipped on the light, but nothing seemed to be out of order. Checking behind the door, the only thing she found was a towel.

Next, she moved toward the second door, knowing that if anyone was hiding in the house, that was the room they'd probably be in. Carefully, she peeked around the corner preparing herself for what she might find.

Holding her breath, she saw an unmade twin bed, an older looking dresser, and a change of clothes on the floor. The house was empty. She reholstered her gun and called the sheriff.

"What's goin' on, Brigid?" he asked as he answered.

"We're too late, something's happened," she said quickly. "Mike's not here, and it seems to me there was a struggle. You better send someone over to collect evidence."

"On it," he said. "Use yer' camera phone to document the scene. Make sure ya' wear gloves if ya' touch anythin'. I'll send someone over right away. See if a neighbor or anyone saw anythin'. Call me when yer' done." He hung up quickly and Brigid began to take photos of the house with her phone.

From what she could tell, the struggle happened in the archway area between the living room and the kitchen. Mike may have been preparing a salad and heard a noise. She took closeups of the knife and the statue. Then she moved to the kitchen and began to look around there. First she took a general snapshot of the room, then she moved closer to the counter where the veggies were.

She took a picture of them, hoping it would help to give them a rough estimate of when this had taken place. From the looks of the lettuce, carrots, and green peppers, it couldn't have been too long ago. They looked slightly dry, as if they'd been sitting out for less than an hour, which was good, because that meant that whatever had happened wasn't all that long ago.

Brigid moved on to the open drawer nearby and noticed that there was a packet of zip ties inside it. A couple of them were sticking up above the drawer, as if someone had been in a hurry and pulled a few from the packet. She took a photo of them just as she heard a car pull up outside. Hurrying to the door, she saw it was the department's only female officer, Deputy Keegan.

"Brigid," she said with a nod as she stepped inside. "What do we have here?"

"From what I can tell, I'd say that Mike Loomis was abducted," Brigid began. "There's no body and no blood. The doors were open, and it looks like there may have been a struggle," she said as she pointed towards the knife and statue. "There's an open drawer in the kitchen that looks as though zip ties were taken from it."

Deputy Keegan nodded. "I'd say that's a fair assumption. From the looks of these other drawers, our suspect pulled them open and then partially shut them when he didn't find what he was looking for."

"I agree," Brigid said. "I think I should go talk to the neighbors and see if anyone noticed anything useful."

"Good idea," Deputy Keegan said. "If we can get a description of the getaway vehicle and the perp, that would be great. With any luck, someone was outside doing yard work when this happened. I'm going to double check the house and then search the yard for more clues. If they did kidnap him, it looks like they wanted him alive, but I'm willing to bet we're working on borrowed time."

"You're probably right," Brigid said. "Mike was worried that some of the people he used to associate with when he was dealing drugs were watching him. If they thought he was talking to the police, they might have taken him to find out what he'd told the authorities."

"And once they get the information they're looking for, they aren't exactly going to just bring him back home with a pat on the head and wish him good luck," Deputy Keegan finished.

"We have to find him before they decide they don't need him anymore," Brigid said in a determined voice. "He's trying to turn his life around. He can't lose it after all of this."

"He won't," Deputy Keegan said confidently. "We've got this. Go see what you can dig up."

CHAPTER TWELVE

Brigid walked outside and looked around at Mike's neighbors' homes. She tried to figure out which one might have someone home. There was one that had a "For Sale" sign in the front yard and an empty driveway. Most likely, no one was there. The next one had a single car in the driveway, but the curtains were drawn. Still, she thought she better try it. While she was deciding what to do, she saw a woman cautiously walking toward her.

"I'm sorry to intrude," the woman began. She looked to be in her late fifties, and had gardening kneepads on over her jeans. A pink sun visor was nestled in her dark, curly hair, and she was wearing gardening gloves that were coated with dirt. "But is something wrong?"

Brigid took in the woman's appearance and felt a sliver of hope. "My name is Brigid Olsen, and I'm with the sheriff's department. It looks like the person living in this house has gone missing and we're looking into his disappearance,

"Did you happen to see anyone coming or going from this house before I showed up?" If the woman had been outside long enough to get that dirty, maybe she'd at least heard something.

"Well, yes, actually I did," she said, placing one hand on her hip. "I saw a cleaner's van pull up over here," she said, motioning towards the street in front of the house where Mike Loomis lived.

"A cleaner's van?" Brigid asked.

"Yeah, you know those vans that have crews that come in and really clean your place for you? They do the carpets and all kinds of heavy-duty stuff. I can't remember the name of the company, but I'd know it if I saw it," she explained. "It was dark blue with white letters."

Brigid nodded. "I know the one you're talking about. They're an out-of-town business, but they're pretty popular here in Cottonwood Springs. Super Cleaners, right?"

"That's it," the woman said, nodding.

"Could you tell me your name?" Brigid asked.

"Marsha Lawton," she said quickly. "Forgive me, I thought I'd mentioned it."

"Not a problem," Brigid assured her. "Would you mind telling me exactly what you saw?"

"Sure," Marsha said with a nod. "I was out here by the side of the house, kind of tucked behind that bush over there," she explained as she pointed towards a bush between the driveway and the house.

"I was doing the last of my weeding and such, getting ready for the change in seasons. Anyhoo, the van pulled up in front of the house over there, and a man climbed out of the driver's side and walked up to it. I thought it was kind of odd that he wasn't in uniform and that there was only one guy, not a whole crew, but I just sort of shrugged it off."

"What did he look like?" Brigid asked. "Anything you can tell me about him will help."

Marsha nodded. "Well, I didn't get a good look at his face. He was wearing a hooded jacket and a puffy vest over it. The hood was pulled up on his head, and I'm almost certain he had a hat or something on under that. I thought it was kind of odd, because I didn't think it was that cool out, but since I'd been working in the yard for a while, I figured I'd just warmed up a bit."

"So you couldn't see his hair or his skin color?" Brigid asked, trying not to sound disappointed.

"The woman shook her head. "No, I'm sorry. I think he may have been dark, but I'm not certain. He could have just been really tan. Hard to say for sure."

"Well, that's better than nothing," Brigid told her. "Every little detail helps. So he got out of the van and walked up to the house?" she prompted.

"Yes. Because of the way he was parked, I couldn't see what happened when he got to the door, but I wasn't paying all that much attention to him. Mind you, I just glanced at him a couple of times."

She pulled a glove off and tapped her chin. "I went back to my weeding, and I hummed a song or two before I heard the van start up. I looked up and saw it pull up into the driveway. The sun was bright, so it was hard for me to see inside it. The person pulled around to the back of the house and parked there for a while."

"You think the man wasn't in the house very long, maybe five or ten minutes, before he pulled the van around in back?" Brigid asked.

"Yeah, something like that," Marsha agreed. "It could have been a little less, though. I'm not real sure."

"Okay," Brigid nodded. "When he pulled around in back, you weren't able to see the van anymore, would that be right?"

"Yes," she said. "I just thought he was going to carry his cleaning stuff in through the back," she explained. "But it really wasn't that long before he left. I'd gone inside my house to get a glass of iced tea when I heard the van start up. I walked over to the window to see what was going on, but I just caught the back end of the van. Lucky number 13."

"Excuse me?" Brigid asked, confused. "What do you mean?"

"Oh, the van number. You know when companies have multiple vehicles, they put numbers on them? This one was number 13. It was right on the back door."

"Really," Brigid said as her mind began to work. "That could be extremely helpful. Thank you, Ms. Lawton. Are you going to be home if we have any more questions?"

"I should be," she said with a nod. "I have to go grocery shopping later on, but that won't be for quite some time, since I still have to make out a grocery list."

"Great," Brigid said quickly. "Thank you so much." She turned away from the woman and headed towards her car. She opened the door and sat down on the seat, so she could pull her notebook from her purse. She wrote down the cleaning company's name and the number 13 along with the skin tone description.

Marsha may have felt like she wasn't helpful, but Brigid knew right away that whoever it was, they had a dark complexion. Although that included a lot of nationalities and even people who were tan, it at least shrunk the possibilities of who the man was. So did the list of people Mike had given Brigid the last time she'd spoken with him.

She pulled her phone out of her purse and dialed the sheriff.

"What ya' got?" he asked when he answered his phone.

"Whoever took Mike used a Super Cleaners van, specifically van number 13," Brigid said. "I plan on telling Deputy Keegan, but I figured you could get the ball rolling. There's a witness who saw that particular van pay a visit to Mike that wasn't there long enough to do an actual cleaning job. She didn't get a very good look at the driver.

The only thing she could tell was that it was a darker skinned male."

"That's okay," he said. "Whoever it was probably was ensurin' it was harder to see him at the house. Maybe he wasn't quite so careful when he took the van. I'll call over and talk to them about surveillance footage. Anythin' else?"

"Not yet," Brigid said. "But Deputy Keegan is combing the house and yard for evidence. I also have the list of people Mike gave me the other day that he said he was worried about."

"Good," he said, sounding satisfied. "When she's done, have Keegan take ya' to the station. I want ya' to help her look through the criminal records database. Maybe some of these guys Mike was worried 'bout got priors, so they'll be in the system. Might give us an idea what these people look like."

"Will do," Brigid said. "I need to go back in the house and see what Deputy Keegan has found."

"All right. Lemme' know if ya' need anythin'," he said before he ended the call. Brigid climbed back out of her car and headed into the house. Deputy Keegan had been hard at work documenting and collecting evidence. She was standing on the back porch, looking closely at the stairs.

"Did you find something out here?" Brigid asked.

"It looks like this was how he was carried out," she said. "I'd say he was knocked out, zip tied, and then drug or carried to a waiting vehicle that was over there."

Deputy Keegan pointed to the end of the driveway that curved behind the house. "You can tell from the scuff marks left by his heels. And I'm pretty sure they used that to prop the door open," she said, as she pointed to a nearby brick.

"It was a Super Cleaners van," Brigid supplied. "I told the sheriff about it, and he's contacting them as we speak."

"Good," Deputy Keegan said. "He's quicker at getting information than I'd be. Did your witness see who did it?"

"Not very well," Brigid said as she shook her head. "But I do have a list of people Mike Loomis was worried about."

"Excellent. At least we aren't just shooting in the dark," she said as she scanned the back yard. "I found a boot print over there, but it seems to be about average size. Still, it might be of some help. You never know."

"You never know is right," Brigid agreed. "I'm going to check with the rest of the neighbors, just in case anyone else happened to see something or was outside."

Deputy Keegan nodded. "I'll finish up with the crime scene. It shouldn't take me too much longer, and then we can head to the station."

Brigid agreed and began walking back to the front of the house. Excluding the house that was for sale and the neighbor she'd already spoken to, there were still a handful of houses she needed to contact. With any luck, maybe someone else saw something more than Marsha had. That would make this whole thing much easier.

If not, she crossed her fingers that they could figure out who it was with enough time to find Mike. She didn't want whoever had taken him to decide to get rid of him. Then, no matter what they found, it would be too late.

CHAPTER THIRTEEN

Brigid spoke to the rest of the neighbors, but none of them had noticed anything more than a van pulling up. Disappointed, she'd met Deputy Keegan near her patrol vehicle and told her she'd follow her to the station. When they met there, they sat down at the deputy's desk to search the criminal records database.

"Okay, here's the database," the deputy said as she clicked on an icon on the desktop of her computer. "Who's the first person you have on your list?"

"Luis Lopez," Brigid said. "Mike mentioned him and Jesse Stanford."

"I've heard of Jesse Stanford," Deputy Keegan said. "And none of it was good."

"Oh?" Brigid asked. "Like what?" She knew what Mike had said, but still, it was interesting to see what someone else, particularly a sheriff's deputy, had heard.

"He's slippery and on the bad team," she surmised. "Here, look." She'd brought up an online file showing that he'd been arrested a number of times, but had never been convicted. He was suspected of selling drugs out of his club in Denver as well as supplying lots of smaller dealers. His arrests had been for battery, arson, breaking and entering, and numerous other things, but the authorities had not been able to make the charges stick.

"Is there a good picture of him?" Brigid asked as they scrolled through the information. "Something fairly recent?"

"Here's one from online. It shows it's from three days ago," Deputy Keegan said as she enlarged the photo.

"Well, he looks dark-skinned," Brigid pointed out. "Looks like he must be using a tanning spray or something like that."

"I agree with you," the deputy said. "I've seen pictures of him before, and I don't remember him being that dark."

"That means he's still a suspect," Brigid said as she started a new list. "But with him being based in Denver, I'd think it would be hard for him to just pop over and snatch Mike."

"True," Deputy Keegan said. "But you mentioned Luis Lopez, right? He's worked for Jesse for quite some time. If Luis did it, Jesse was probably behind it." She leaned back in her chair and sighed.

"It would be amazing to put Jesse Stanford behind bars. It's like, we all know the guy's dirty, but he just keeps slipping through everyone's fingers. It'd be a nice win for our department if we could be the ones to actually make something stick on him."

She leaned forward again and typed in Luis Lopez's name. "Luis hasn't caused much trouble in recent years, but he has a number of battery charges from earlier. Once he went under Jesse's wing, and because Jesse is so influential, Luis became just as untouchable. Here he is." She brought up a picture of Luis.

"He's dark, too," Brigid sighed.

"Yep, and honestly, they all could be this time of year. Since we're coming out of summer, if these guys spent any time in the sun, they'll probably be dark enough to qualify," Deputy Keegan said sadly.

"Good point," Brigid said, "but let's print out their addresses and any other contact info we might need while we're at it."

"Done," the deputy said after a couple of clicks. "Luis lives in Denver, so he'd need some travel time, too," she pointed out.

"The next one is a Derek Walden," Brigid read from her notes.

Deputy Keegan typed in his name and waited for the results. "Doesn't look like we've got much on him other than a couple of fairly basic citations. Wonder if this guy's in the wrong crowd?" She asked as she pulled up his picture. "From what I'm seeing, he looks like your average joe."

"It's one of the names Mike gave me. But who knows? Maybe the guy doesn't do that sort of thing anymore. After all, it's been a while since Mike was dealing. Let me look at my notes again." She scanned through them and shook her head.

"This guy is supposedly the one who picked up where Mike left off after he was arrested. Mike heard this is the guy you call when you want something illegal. He wondered if this Derek guy saw his release from prison as a threat and wanted to scare Mike off."

"That's certainly not out of the realm of possibility," Deputy Keegan said. "I've seen that happen before. These people can get very territorial. If they so much as think that you're trying to take business away from them, things can get ugly.

"He doesn't live in Cottonwood Springs, either," Brigid said as she began to think. "I have an idea, but I'll wait until we look at the last one. Jeremy Duggins is his name," she said.

After the deputy did a little typing, his name finally came up.

"He doesn't have a criminal record," Deputy Keegan read. "But our records do show a few things for him. Addresses and such."

"Maybe this guy's just been lucky and hasn't gotten caught,"

Brigid said with a shrug.

"What was Mike's reason for naming him?" Deputy Keegan asked.

"I guess he and Mike used to help each other out from time to time. But the thing is, Mike saw Jeremy driving by his house not too long ago. Apparently Mike was standing in the doorway of his house when his parole officer was leaving, and he saw Jeremy drive by," Brigid said.

"Although the guy may not have a record, that doesn't mean anything," Deputy Keegan said. "I mean, he could just be good at staying off our radar. If Mike said he used to deal drugs, I'm sure he did, but this guy may just be smarter than Mike was."

"And all of them have a motive to keep Mike quiet if they thought he was talking to law enforcement officials," Brigid pointed out.

"Yep, and my guess is that whoever did this jumped to conclusions. Mike did get an early release, but that was for good behavior. They probably saw his parole officer or something and assumed he'd ratted someone out for his freedom."

Deputy Keegan leaned back in her chair. "Well, two of them are in Denver, and the other two don't live in Cottonwood Springs, but in nearby towns. What was your idea?"

"Oh!" Brigid said, almost forgetting. "We know they used a Super Cleaners van. I remember from the commercials they have a couple of locations. My thought was to find out which location that van came from and approach the person who is closest to it."

"That could work," Deputy Keegan said with a nod. "And hopefully the cleaning company had security cameras that can show us who took the van. With any luck they were a little sloppier there than when they were at Mike's."

Her cell phone began to ring, and she smiled when she saw the

ID. "Speak of the devil, it's the sheriff." She answered and listened intently. "Yeah, Brigid's right here. We've been going over possible suspects in the database." She paused and listened. "Can you forward the video to us once you get it?"

Brigid was listening intently to what she could hear of the conversation. Her guess was that Sheriff Davis had narrowed down which location the van had come from.

"Will do," Deputy Keegan said. "I'll update you if we find out more. See you soon." She ended the call and turned to Brigid. "The van is out of Evergreen Hills, which, as you can see from what we turned up, is where Jeremy Duggins is from."

"So either he did it," Brigid began, "or one of the other two stopped off there and grabbed it." She pointed to the map she'd brought up on her phone. "You have to go through Evergreen Hills to get to Denver, and it's just a little detour to Casey Park, where Derek lives."

"Yes, you're right," Deputy Keegan said. "Although right now everyone is still a possible suspect, I'd like to check out Duggins first. Sheriff Davis said that he'd be heading back here in the next couple of hours. Since we have people from Denver on our list, he wanted to make sure he was present when they were approached. He'll have to notify the Denver Police Department and protocol will have to be followed."

Brigid nodded. "I figured as much. Still, we can go talk to Jeremy and Derek while we wait for him to return. Who knows? Maybe we can find Mike Loomis before he gets back." She knew she was being optimistic considering what they had to work with, but she had to stay positive.

"Maybe, but I wouldn't have my heart set on it," Deputy Keegan said. "Still, we can take a ride over to Evergreen Hills. That's in our jurisdiction. Let's go."

CHAPTER FOURTEEN

Brigid and Deputy Keegan climbed into Deputy Keegan's car and began to buckle up.

"I'll tell you one thing, Brigid, I have a feeling this is going to end up being bigger than we imagine," Deputy Keegan sighed as she started the car.

"Why do you say that, Deputy?" Brigid asked as they pulled out of the sheriff's station parking lot.

Deputy Keegan smiled. "Please call me Lindsey. And I don't know, just a hunch, I guess."

"Well, whatever happens, I hope we find Mike safe and sound. I know he used to be involved in illegal things, but I don't feel people's past mistakes should be held over them. If he's really turned over a new leaf, I wish all the best for him."

Brigid truly hoped Mike had changed his ways. There was nothing sadder than to see a person who couldn't stay out of trouble. It seemed as though some people were just determined to stay on the wrong side of the law. She hoped Mike wasn't one of them.

"I hope so too," Deputy Keegan said. "But in this line of work, it's hard to remain positive when it comes to stuff like that."

"I'm sure," Brigid said. "Is Cottonwood Springs where you got your start?"

"No, I used to live in Denver. I started out as an officer there, but I didn't like being a police officer in a big city. When I saw the employment listing for the sheriff's department here in Cottonwood Springs, I thought it was a good change of pace. I'm glad I came." She gave Brigid a smile. "I think I was more of a country girl than I realized."

"There's something peaceful about the area, that's for sure," Brigid agreed.

A little while later, they pulled up to an apartment complex in Evergreen Hills, which consisted of three buildings with roughly eight apartments each. The grey siding had seen better days, and the concrete in front of them was cracked and crumbling. The apartments may have been nice at one time, but now they had a rundown and sad look to them.

"This doesn't look like the greatest neighborhood," Brigid commented as she unbuckled her seatbelt.

"No, it doesn't," Deputy Keegan said. "And I'm willing to bet most folks here aren't going to be a big fan of me showing up." She leaned forward and peered out her windshield at the kids glaring at them from the balcony above.

"I think you're right. Looks like we better find Jeremy before word spreads," Brigid said as she opened the car door. Thankfully, it didn't take long before they found his apartment and knocked.
"I'm going to stand a little out of view," Deputy Keegan said. "We don't want him thinking we're here to arrest him or something."

Brigid nodded and did her best to stand in front of the peephole in the door, just in case Jeremy Duggins decided to look through it before opening his door. After a moment, she heard the locks disengage on the door, and a man pulled it open. She saw his eyes dart over her shoulder, and he swallowed nervously. She was sure he was trying to look calm, but she noticed the small little tells that said he wasn't comfortable.

"Can I help you?" he asked.

"Hello, my name is Brigid Olsen," she said as she held her hand out. "Are you Jeremy Duggins?"

"I am," he said as he shook her hand. He then nodded towards Deputy Keegan. "What's with the officer?"

"Deputy Keegan," Lindsay said as she stepped forward.

"We're trying to get some information on a man named Mike Loomis," Brigid said, and she noticed that Jeremy swallowed heavily when Mike's name was mentioned. "You aren't in any trouble, but he may be. May we come in and talk to you? I promise it won't take long."

He hesitated, clearly debating whether he should let them in. Finally, he nodded and stepped outside. "We can talk over there where the benches are," he said, nodding toward a few benches next to a playground.

"Fine by me," Brigid shrugged as she looked over at Deputy Keegan. She nodded and followed them over to the benches.

"How did you get my name?" he asked. "Mike been talking or what?"

"Well, something like that," Brigid began. "He's been having problems at his house, and I spoke with him about it a few days ago. I'm not an officer, but I work with the sheriff's department. Someone was harassing him, and he believed it was someone from his past. He gave me a list of names of people that he'd either suspected or he'd seen over the last week or two. I don't think he suspected you, but it was more that he'd seen you, if I remember correctly."

"He did," Jeremy said as he relaxed slightly. When they got to the black benches, they sat down. "I was in Cottonwood Springs not too long ago." He hesitated a moment and then he said, "Am I under arrest or something?" he asked.

"Not at all," Deputy Keegan said. "We're just here for questions. Mike Loomis is missing, and we're trying to figure if someone might have taken him."

"Oh," he said, suddenly realizing the severity of the situation. "What do you mean, he's missing?"

"Well, right now all I can tell you for certain is that when I went to his house to speak with him this morning, the doors were wide open, and it looked as though there may have been a struggle. We've tried to get in contact with him, but nothing. With the other things that have happened, we think he was kidnapped," Brigid said. Deputy Keegan nodded.

"We can't tell you a whole lot more since it's an open investigation. But we were hoping that you could give us some information and help us fill in the blanks," Deputy Keegan said. Brigid nodded. She wasn't sure if they should tell him about what had happened before Mike had disappeared. After all, as far as they knew, Jeremy did it.

"When did he go missing?" he finally asked.

"This morning. We're still trying to peg down an actual time, but we think it was around 8:30," Brigid said.

"Wow, I was out eating breakfast while the dude was getting snatched from his own house?" Jeremy shook his head.

"You were eating breakfast somewhere?" Deputy Keegan asked. "Can you prove that?"

"Are you serious?" he asked. "What you mean is that you want to make sure I didn't take him, right?" He began digging in his pocket. "I've got a receipt in here somewhere." He pulled it out and handed it to Brigid. "See, I was at the Green Street Cafe at 8:29 a.m."

Brigid looked at the receipt and nodded. "Good. We just have to cover all of our bases. The vehicle he was taken in came from here in Evergreen Hills. With you living here…"

"Hey, I get it," he said. "You got to do your job and all that. Man, I can't believe someone would do that."

"You wouldn't have any idea who it could have been, would you?" Brigid asked. "Anything you can think of might help us to bring him home safe."

"Look, Mike used to be wrapped up with some serious dudes, that's all I know. As to names and stuff like that, I never had a clue, and I wanted to keep it that way. With the things Mike was doing, I figured the less I knew, the better." Jeremy was clearly uncomfortable talking about Mike's line of work, and Brigid had a pretty good idea why.

Brigid turned to Deputy Keegan and said, "It looks like Jeremy has told us everything he knows. I want to have a few words with him privately. Why don't I meet you at the car?"

Lindsey looked from her to Jeremy and then back again. "Sure," she said with a nod. "Nice to meet you, Mr. Duggins. I hope if we meet again it's in better circumstances." He returned the nod, and she walked towards her car.

"I just want to tell you, that if you're into some illegal line of work, you might want to consider changing it," Brigid began.

"I don't do anything…," he began, but she cut him off.

"Look, Mike didn't like giving me your name, and he told me he wasn't even sure if you were still selling. But you seem like a smart kid, and I'd hate to see you get wrapped up in something like this. I just wanted to say that I'll be praying for you. And if you're the praying type, maybe you should pray for Mike."

Brigid let her words sink in. Jeremy seemed surprised that a stranger would say such a thing to him.

"Thank you," he said finally. "I haven't prayed in a long time, but maybe I should."

Brigid didn't know why she'd felt compelled to say what she'd just said, but she decided to continue. "I don't pray much either," she admitted. "But lately I've been seeing more and more people that just need someone to put in a good word for them. I don't believe that most people are inherently bad, they've just started down the wrong path in life. Sometimes all they need is for someone to shine a light for them to find their way."

"My grandmama used to say that," he said softly, his voice catching. "She used to tell me 'do your best Jeremy. You never know when someone might need your light to find their way.' I'd totally forgotten about that. She's been gone almost ten years now."

"The world works in mysterious ways," Brigid said as she stood up. "You have a good day, Mr. Duggins."

"You too, Mrs. Olsen. And thank you. I'll put in a good word with the big man upstairs for Mike," he said as he stayed seated on the bench.

Brigid nodded and turned away, heading for the car. As she made her way toward Deputy Keegan, she noticed she was talking on her phone.

"That was Sheriff Davis," she told Brigid. "He spoke with an employee at Super Cleaners here in town. She said the company didn't think they could send the footage, but we should go there and take a look at it."

Brigid nodded. "Sounds good. Let's head over there now."

Both women climbed in the car and pulled away. Brigid noticed that Jeremy Duggins was still sitting on the metal bench.

Unbeknownst to her, he was thinking about what Brigid had said. Her words had moved him so much, they'd shaken him to his core.

CHAPTER FIFTEEN

"Here we are," Deputy Keegan said as they pulled up in front of the Super Cleaners.

"It's not as big as I expected it to be," Brigid said as they climbed out of Keegan's patrol car. "But I guess you don't need a big space when you're always going to the clients' homes."

They entered the building and Brigid instantly felt the tension in the air. A man, who looked like he was the manager, was standing in front of a young female employee with his arms crossed over his chest. The woman looked worried as she turned and saw Brigid and Deputy Keegan enter.

"Hello, we're with the Cottonwood Springs Sheriff's Department. Evidently the sheriff talked to someone from here, and they said we could look at some security camera footage."

"Yes, and you better make it quick," the man said firmly as he straightened his tie. It was apparent he was trying to control his anger. "I don't want the sheriff's department sniffing around and ruining my business."

"I assure you sir, we'll be quick. We won't cause any trouble for you," Deputy Keegan said.

The man made an indignant noise and disappeared through a door behind him.

"Sorry about that," the employee said. "I didn't think he'd get so bent out of shape over this."

"Why is he so mad?" Brigid asked. "By the way, I'm Brigid and this is Deputy Keegan."

"I'm Chelsea," the young woman said. "I don't know why he's mad. I answered the phone and told the sheriff that I'd bring the footage up on our computer. After I talked to him, I told the manager you'd be coming here to look at it. When I told him, he just blew up and started yelling that he didn't want you sniffing around, and if he told you no now it would look like he was hiding something." She shrugged her shoulders like she was confused.

"Well, that's an odd thing to say," Deputy Keegan said.

"Yeah, I agree," Chelsea said. "I mean, like why is it such a big deal to him, but honestly, I think he's a little shady."

"Oh?" Brigid asked. "What do you mean?"

"Now, keep in mind I haven't worked here very long, okay?" she began. "There could be a good explanation for it. I don't know, but I've seen a lot of TV crime shows, and it looks to me like this guy is in with some sort of mob or something."

"Why would you think that?" Deputy Keegan asked, suddenly interested.

"For one thing, who doesn't want to show security camera footage to law enforcement? Especially if one of your vans was stolen, and you didn't know about it? I mean, I'm assuming it was used in a crime, right?" the woman asked.

"But there's been other stuff too. Like strange guys coming here and having secret meetings with him. Mr. Phillips looked just as nervous when the guy showed up as when you did. Plus, some of the cleaners have told me that they end up going into the city to do jobs, even though that's out of our area. I mean, why not just get someone local?"

"That is odd," Brigid admitted. "But nothing we can really do anything about."

"Yeah, I know," Chelsea said. "Still it's weird. Anyway, here's that film footage." She clicked a few keys on her computer and brought it up. "See, the guy walks right up and climbs in the van like he owns it."

What she said was true. On the footage, the person walked up to the van and climbed inside. Almost immediately, he started the van and backed it out of its parking space.

"Is it normal to leave the keys in the vans?" Deputy Keegan asked.

"No," Chelsea whispered, shaking her head. "But the manager told me to tell you that we do." She looked towards the door the man had gone through.

"What usually happens?" Brigid asked quietly.

"The keys are inside the building, and the vans are locked. But as you can see, whoever took the van knew which one would be unlocked and that the keys would be in it." Chelsea leaned back and said, "Seems odd, doesn't it?"

"It sounds to me like your manager is in on it," Brigid whispered. "Are there any other cameras?"

"No, and when I came in today, Mr. Phillips was at this computer. He tried to act like he wasn't doing anything, but I could see that he'd exited from wherever he'd been on it."

"Go back and see if you can find out who put the keys in the van," Deputy Keegan muttered.

Chelsea nodded and began rewinding the footage on screen. "Wait, did you see that?"

Brigid shook her head, "No what?"

"The time jumped," Chelsea said as she pointed to the time stamp. Sure enough, there was a point when ten minutes of the footage was missing.

"Sure looks like he tampered with it," Brigid said.

"Yes and no," Deputy Keegan muttered. "But it's not good enough. He could always claim it was the system glitching or something. I've seen it before. My guess is, he was erasing the footage and you came in before he could finish it."

"Yes, that makes sense," Chelsea said.

"Play it again. I'd like to see if we can get a better view of the thief's face," Brigid said.

Chelsea found the spot again and slowly inched it forward. "There, I think that's the best you're going to get," she said.

The three of them peered at the blurry screen. Deputy Keegan shook her head. "You can tell by the build that it's a man. His skin isn't terribly dark, so that rules out the suspect we already knew had an alibi. But since the image is in black and white as well as being grainy, that's all we have."

"Sorry," Chelsea said. "I wish it was better."

"Me too," Deputy Keegan said. "From the angle of it, it's hard to even estimate his height. Plus, with that hood pulled over his head, we can't determine his hair color."

"Now what?" Brigid asked.

"I think we're done here," Deputy Keegan said loudly. The other two could tell she was doing it for the sake of Mr. Phillips, the manager. She leaned over and slid something across the desk to Chelsea. "Here's my card. If you see him doing anything you think is suspicious, call or text me. That's my direct number."

Chelsea nodded. "I will. I'll probably be searching for a new job, too," she sighed.

"I think that would be smart," Brigid said. "Good luck."

Deputy Keegan and Brigid left the building and stepped out into the sunshine. It was starting to warm up outside and the sun was intense, especially for this time of year.

"What do you think about what we just saw?" Brigid asked as they got back in Deputy Keegan's patrol car.

"There's definitely something going on with him," Deputy Keegan mused. "I'd be willing to bet he's in with whoever did this. Maybe he doesn't know what they specifically did, but he certainly gave them the means to do it."

"Which would make him an accomplice," Brigid said. "So why not arrest him?"

"On what grounds?" Deputy Keegan asked. "I mean, sure, we could say he tampered with the video, but that's circumstantial. Really, anything that we could use would be flimsy at best. I think it's better to let him think we aren't onto him. Then, we find the guy who did it and get him to admit the manager's involvement."

Brigid looked around at the neighboring businesses as they circled the parking lot. "I wonder if any of these other places have camera footage that might show who put the keys in the van?"

"That's a good idea. We can always look into that later, depending on what we find out," Deputy Keegan said. She paused as her phone made a noise indicating she had a text on it. "It's Sheriff Davis," she said. "He wants us to meet him at Mike Loomis' house and walk him through what we have so far. It looks like he's back."

"Good, then he can start contacting whoever he needs to about the suspects in Denver. I'd like to look into that Derek guy and see where he was when Mike disappeared," Brigid said.

"Yes," Deputy Keegan said. "Who is that guy again? Why did Mike think he was behind it?"

"He's supposed to be the new drug dealer who took Mike's place. From what Mike told me, these people can get territorial," Brigid shrugged.

"That they do," Deputy Keegan said. "I've seen some serious stuff happen over that sort of thing. Most of them are pretty laid back and don't want to stir up trouble, but there are others that just seem to be spoiling for a fight." She pulled her car out into traffic.

"I hope he's not too hard to find," Brigid said as she gazed out of the passenger window. "Otherwise we might have our work cut out for us."

"Well, we'll soon find out," she said. "If we have to, we'll talk to the local police there and see if they have any tips for us. If they've dealt with him before, they may have an idea where to find him and how to approach him."

"Good thinking," Brigid said with a smile. "You know, I kind of like working with you."

"I was just thinking the same thing," Deputy Keegan said.

CHAPTER SIXTEEN

"I'm sorry you had to cut your trip short, but I'm glad you're back," Deputy Keegan said to Sheriff Davis as they climbed out of her car. They had just pulled up in front of Mike Loomis' house, and Sheriff Davis had walked over to their car. As he did so, he seemed to be taking in every single blade of grass and leaf on the ground, wishing they could tell him what had happened to Mike Loomis.

"I'm not sorry," he said. "Things weren't workin' out as planned, anyway." He shot a look at Brigid, and she had a feeling she knew what he was talking about. She gathered his date didn't go as well as he would have liked for it to, which was too bad, because she was really hoping he'd have a woman in his life that he cared about. He deserved it. "Okay. Break it down fer me."

"I arrived at Mike's house this morning to talk to him about having someone officially watch him," Brigid began. "When I went to the door it was standing partially open. I entered the house and saw what looked like signs of a struggle."

He followed her inside and she pointed out what she'd seen. The knife and statue were no longer on the ground. They'd been tagged and collected as evidence. She continued to explain what she found and then let Deputy Keegan take over from her.

"Gatherin' ya' went to Evergreen Hills," he said as he looked over at them.

"Yes, we did. We were there questioning a possible suspect when you phoned us about the security camera footage," Deputy Keegan said.

"And I take it he weren't our guy since we're still investigatin'," he said, staring at something behind them.

"Yes, sir. That's correct," she said as she watched him closely. "What are you looking at?"

"Don't turn around, either of you," he began. "But there's a car parked along the street that's been there since before I got here, and someone's sittin' in the driver's seat. My eyesight ain't what it used to be, but I'd almost be willin' to bet money they're watchin' us."

"You want me to check it out?" Deputy Keegan asked.

"Yeah. Keep hidden until ya' know for sure. It's that l'il grey rust bucket parked behind the black SUV," he said. "Brigid, ya' stay here and keep talkin' to me."

Deputy Keegan walked toward the back of the house and disappeared.

"So I'm guessing that things didn't go well on your trip," Brigid said, striking up a conversation with him.

"Nope," he said sadly. "But I guess that happens. Sometimes people ain't who we think they are."

"There are still plenty of other options out there," Brigid said gently. "You might be surprised when you finally find her. Maybe she's been here in Cottonwood Springs the whole time, and you just overlooked her."

"Doubt it," he said with a sigh. "But like ya' said, I'm jes' gonna' keep my options open. It'd be nice to settle down and have a family.

Ain't getting' any younger."

"You'll find the one who's right for you. I have faith in that," Brigid said with a smile.

"Keegan's comin' up behind the car. Don't look like he's noticed her yet," Sheriff Davis said, changing the subject. "Man, if she ain't a slick one. Nothin' much she can't do."

"I hadn't met her before. When did she start?" Brigid asked.

"Not too long ago," he said.

Suddenly, there was a loud commotion, and Brigid heard Deputy Keegan yell. "Freeze, don't move another inch!"

"I wasn't doing anything, I swear!" The man yelled back.

Brigid turned and saw Deputy Keegan putting the man in handcuffs.

"If you weren't doing nothin', why have ya' been sittin' in yer' car watchin' me for the past twenty minutes?" Sheriff Davis asked as he walked over to them.

"Maybe I'm just keeping an eye on you," the man sneered.

When Sheriff Davis, who was wearing civilian clothes, got to them, he pulled his badge out. "That's odd considerin' I'm the law 'round here, and ya' just tried to run from one of my deputies. Let's try this again, what are ya' doin'?" He led the man over to the side of the road.

"Man, I wasn't doing anything," the guy said.

Deputy Keegan began to read him his rights while he complained. When she was finished, she asked, "What's your name?"

"I'm not telling you," he said.

"Well then, guess I'll have to search ya'," Sheriff Davis said. "Got anythin' in your pockets we oughtta' know 'bout? Anythin' that's gonna hurt me?" he asked as he began to pat the man down.

"I've got a pocket knife," the man said, starting to calm down. "It's in my right pocket."

Sheriff Davis reached into the man's back pocket and pulled out his wallet. "Derek Walden," he read. "Why are ya' sittin' on the side of the road in my town when ya' don't even live here, Derek?"

"He's one of our suspects," Brigid said quickly.

"Well now, ain't that interestin'," Sheriff Davis said with a smile as if he'd just heard the best news of the day.

"What?" Derek asked. "A suspect in what?"

"The disappearance of Mike Loomis," Sheriff Davis said. "And here yer' sittin' outside his house and runnin' away from my officer."

"I, I, I didn't do anything wrong," Derek sputtered. "I don't even know the guy."

"And yet, here you are," Deputy Keegan said as she crossed her arms. "If I were you, I'd start being real honest, real fast."

Sheriff Davis continued to search Derek's' pockets. He pulled out the pocket knife and a baggy with a white powder in it. "Looks like your day is 'bout to get worse," Sheriff Davis said as he lifted the bag in the air. "What's this gonna' come back as when I test it?"

"Man, you know what it is. It's coke," Derek sighed.

"This isn't looking good for you," Brigid said softly. "Do you have anything else illegal on you or in your car?"

"There's more in the car," Derek said, deflated.

"Thank ya' for being honest," Sheriff Davis said. "Now, tell me where ya' were this mornin' around 8:30."

"At 8:30?" Derek repeated. "I was over at my girlfriend's house. I spent the night there."

"What are you doing here, Derek?" Deputy Keegan asked. "Give us a real answer this time."

"All right," he sighed. "I was going to rough the guy up a bit. I heard he was out of prison and wanted to get back into the game again. I just wanted to let him know that it wouldn't be smart. I hadn't been here long when you showed up," he said nodding to Sheriff Davis. "I thought maybe you were looking for a hookup, so I stuck around to see if he'd supply you."

"You shoulda' stayed at your girlfriend's, Derek," Sheriff Davis said. "Now I gotta' book you on possession and runnin' from an officer."

"Hey, I didn't run far. I stopped," he pointed out.

"That's true," Sheriff Davis said. "And maybe Deputy Keegan will make a note of that in her report. But fer now, ya' gotta' go to the station." he nodded to Deputy Keegan, and she led him to her car. After he got into the back seat, she shut the door.

"Guess this means he's not our suspect either," Brigid said.

"Probably not," Sheriff Davis said. "Good news is, we're goin' to the station, and I can get ahold of them Denver lawmen. Talked to them a little earlier this mornin'. I tol' 'em some of the situation, but since there were other suspects, said I'd let 'em know. Guess it's time to let 'em know."

"I'll see you two at the station," Deputy Keegan called out to them as she drove by and they nodded.

"Looks like yer' ridin' with me," Sheriff Davis said.

CHAPTER SEVENTEEN

Once Deputy Keegan had Derek booked and locked in a cell, she met the sheriff and Brigid in his office.

"I'm gonna' put some detective with the Denver PD on the speaker, but I want ya' two to stay quiet," he explained. "Jes' don't wanna' have to repeat what he tells me."

Brigid and Deputy Keegan nodded as Sheriff Davis dialed the number. After a moment, he was on the line with the detective in Denver.

"Detective Baptiste, Sheriff Davis here," he said. "Looks like I'm gonna' need to talk to them people I spoke to ya' 'bout earlier."

"I was afraid of that," the deep voice on the other end of the line said. "I've been working on building a substantial case against one of your suspects, Jesse Stanford, for quite a while now. I recently got an inside man for his operations that I may be able to let you speak with if you can come here to Denver."

Sheriff Davis shot a questioning look at both women and they each nodded. Brigid wasn't sure who they'd be talking to, but this case was getting very interesting. There was no way she wanted to go home now, and besides, Linc and Holly would be busy. The only thing she had to look forward to when she got home was editing a book. A trip to Denver would be a much better way to spend her time.

"Yeah, I can do that. It'll take me a l'il while, though," Sheriff Davis replied.

"I'm going to be here for several more hours. Just get here as soon as you can. Let me know when you're close, and I'll have my contact come to the station so you can talk to him," Detective Baptiste promised.

"Will do," Sheriff Davis said before hanging up. "Well, ladies, guess we're goin' on a road trip."

*****

"Here we are," Sheriff Davis said as they pulled into the Denver Police Department's parking lot.

"I never thought I'd see this place again," Deputy Keegan sighed as they unbuckled their seat belts.

"That's right, you did come from Denver. Was this your station?" Brigid asked.

"Sure was, small world. I never imagined a case from Cottonwood Springs would bring me back here," Deputy Keegan said. They climbed out of the car and started walking toward the police building.

It was several stories tall and had been painted in an institutional gray color. A wing jutted out from the side. In front of the building was a small fountain and flower garden with a few benches scattered around it. Brigid thought it looked like a nice place to sit and relax.

After they passed through the double glass doors, Sheriff Davis led them to the front desk. "I'm Sheriff Davis from Cottonwood Springs and we're here to see Detective Baptiste," he told the man behind the counter.

"I'll let him know you're here. Please, take a seat while I get him," the man said, gesturing toward a small seating area that looked out onto the garden. They took a seat and Brigid gazed at the flowers.

"Makes ya' wonder how Mike Loomis got wrapped up in all of this," Sheriff Davis mused as they waited.

"It is kind of crazy when you think about it," Brigid agreed. "I mean, if this Jesse guy is as bad as he sounds, why would anyone even want to get involved with him?"

"Maybe Mike didn't realize it at the time," Deputy Keegan said.

"Sometimes these guys come across as entirely different than who they really are" Sheriff Davis explained. "And often they don't realize who the real supplier is until they're already in pretty deep. After that, ya' usually ain't got a choice 'bout gettin' out. By then, it's too late, and ya' can't get out."

"That's kind of sad," Brigid said. She couldn't imagine ever selling drugs, but understood that some people saw it as something they had to do to make ends meet. What about those people who do it to provide for their family and wind up caught in some craziness with no idea how to get out of it? She shook her head, feeling sorry for them.

"Sheriff Davis?" a deep voice said. They turned around and saw a broad-shouldered man with a crew cut standing nearby. "Lindsey Keegan?" he asked suddenly. "Is that really you?"

"I had a feeling it was you," she said. "So, you made detective."

"I did," he said with a nod. "Are you here with the sheriff?"

"She is," Sheriff Davis said with a nod. "And so is Brigid. She's a consultant fer us and is also workin' with us on this case."

"Well come on back. I have a room where we can talk," he said with a wave.

Brigid shot Deputy Keegan a look, but she shook her head and mouthed the word, "Later."

They followed Detective Baptiste down a hall. He pushed open a door and said, "In here." Inside there was a long table with a laptop on it and a few file folders spread out. "Please, take a seat," he said.

"We're lookin' at two possible suspects in our case," Sheriff Davis began. "We got a person who's missin' and there were signs of a struggle. Got it narrowed down to two people here in Denver."

"One of whom is Jesse Stanford?" Detective Baptiste asked.

"Yep," Sheriff Davis said. "What can ya' tell us 'bout him?"

"Well, as you've probably discovered, he's a bad guy. Started out small, but he's grown in influence over the years. He's really been on our radar the past couple of years, but so far, we haven't been able to get him for anything. We've heard plenty of stories about him, but nothing we can bring him in for.

"The stories involve him having people roughed up, selling drugs out of his club, that type of thing. He's also suspected in an arson case as well as a few other crimes. Of course, he doesn't do much of it himself these days. He has a group of people that do his dirty work for him. What makes you think he took your guy?"

Deputy Keegan spoke up. "Brigid spoke to the victim before he went missing. His name is Mike Loomis, and he recently got out of prison after doing time for selling drugs. He was being harassed before he disappeared and gave Brigid the names of a few people he thought may have been the culprit."

"And Jesse was on that list," Detective Baptiste said.

"That's correct," Brigid said. "He didn't want to name him, but I convinced him we couldn't help if we didn't know who to look at."

"When it comes to Jesse, there's still no guarantees," the detective said. "He's a slippery sucker, I'll give him that."

"I thought no one slipped through your grasp, Alex?" Deputy Keegan said suddenly.

Detective Baptiste grinned at her. "Oh, don't you worry your pretty little head. I'm working on him." He and Deputy Keegan seemed to be engaged in a staring contest.

Brigid and Sheriff Davis exchanged a look. Both of them had noticed that Deputy Keegan didn't seem to be a huge fan of the detective.

"Ya' mentioned somethin' on the phone 'bout an inside man?" Sheriff Davis said, trying to get the conversation back on track.

"I did," the detective said, as he broke eye contact with Deputy Keegan. "I'm actually fairly proud of this one. He should be here any minute now," he said as he checked the time on his phone.

"How can he help our case?" Brigid asked. She was curious who it was, but figured she'd find out soon enough.

"This person is fairly deep into Stanford's operation, so if he's the one who took your guy, he'll either know about it or know where the guy might be. We haven't been able to talk much, because he only approached us earlier this week." The detective looked proud of that fact.

"So you didn't actually do anything," Deputy Keegan surmised. "You just sat back and let the big fish fall in your lap."

"Hey, it's still my fish, no matter how I caught it," he said happily. "Now I get to use that fish to reel in a whale."

"Is he known for snatchin' people outta' their homes?" Sheriff Davis asked, in an attempt to cut off the bickering between the two officers.

"Not particularly," Detective Baptiste said. "But it seems he's been getting braver. Plus, the contact says he believes Stanford's starting to act erratic. Doing risky things and taking situations a little too far. If that's the case, then who knows?"

"Mike was grabbed from his house in broad daylight," Brigid said suddenly. "I'd describe that as risky."

"That it is," Detective Baptiste said as he turned his attention towards her. "And no one saw anything?"

"A neighbor saw the van that was used, which was taken from Super Cleaners in Evergreen Hills. She couldn't get a good look at the driver, because he was covered by his jacket and hat," Brigid explained.

"And no luck from the Super Cleaners either?" he asked.

"That guy was a little off," Deputy Keegan said. "The employee who helped us told us she thinks the manager had knowledge that the van was going to be used. Mysteriously, the van just happened to be unlocked, the keys were left in it, and a section of the security camera footage was missing."

"How convenient," the detective said.

"Our thoughts exactly. We're hoping to bring him in for aiding and abetting before it's all done," Brigid stated. "We're still trying to put all the pieces together."

"I hope you get him," he said. "I hate it when people think they can do something like that and get away with it." Just then, his phone beeped. "Looks like our guy is here. Give me one second, and I'll go get him."

They all nodded and Detective Baptiste stood and left the room.

"We still haven't even talked to him about Luis Lopez yet," Brigid pointed out. "We'll have to see if his guy can tell us anything about him."

"Sounds like he thinks it's this Jesse guy," Sheriff Davis said.

"Yeah, well, sometimes he jumps to conclusions," Deputy Keegan said softly.

"Don't mean to pry, but what's up with ya' two?" the sheriff asked. "I mean, it's pretty obvious."

"It's a long story. I'll tell you on the way home, I promise," she said.

The door clicked open and Detective Baptiste walked into the room followed by a man wearing a hoodie that partially covered his face, "Sheriff Davis, Deputy Keegan, Brigid, I'd like you to meet Luis Lopez."

Luis pushed his hood back and nodded to them. "Nice to meet you."

CHAPTER EIGHTEEN

"Wait a minute," Brigid said, blinking. "You're the informant?"

"I guess you could say that," Luis said as he sat down at the table with them. Meanwhile, Brigid's mind was reeling. How was it that one of their suspects was an informant and had just walked into the police station? How was this possible?

"Luis Lopez?" Deputy Keegan asked. Brigid noticed that Lindsey seemed a bit taken aback by the revelation as well. "I thought you were Jesse's go-to guy? What could possibly be in it for you to turn on him like this? Surely you're sitting pretty by now."

"I guess you could say that. To a certain extent, I am," Luis began. His dark eyes fell to the table where he began to trace the wood grain with his finger. "But I can't go on working for Jesse anymore. Everything he is getting into and asking of us... it's too much. I know I may not be an upright and law-abiding citizen, but I do have some morals, some integrity. Everyone has a line they aren't willing to cross, you know? He asked me to cross my line in the sand."

"These people are working their own case and they think it involves Jesse," Detective Baptiste explained. "Do you think you can help them?"

"I sure can try," Luis said with a heavy sigh. "As long as you protect me and my family."

"We will," the detective promised.

"What line did he ask ya' to cross?" Sheriff Davis asked. "Sorry, but we gotta' know that we can trust the information ya' give us."

"I get it," Luis said with a nod. "I'd be worried if you just took me at my word. I've worked for Jesse for a long time now, but you have to understand, he's changed. He isn't the man he used to be. Now he's ruthless and cruel. I'm starting to wonder exactly what he's doing. If I didn't know any better, I'd think he was losing his mind.

"He told me he knew I wanted out, and in order to do so, I had to find this dealer who recently got out of prison and kill him. If I killed him, he'd let me and my family go, and he'd set us up financially. We could go wherever we wanted to."

Brigid and Deputy Keegan exchanged a look. "Do you know what the man's name is that he wanted killed or where he's from?" Brigid asked.

"Yes," Luis said. "His name is Mike Loomis, and he's from Cottonwood Springs."

"Luis," Sheriff Davis interrupted. "That's the person we're tryin' to find."

"Really?" Luis asked, surprised. "The guy's already gone missing? And you suspect Jesse?"

"And you," Deputy Keegan said. "After all, you are Jesse's right hand man."

"It wasn't me," Luis said, shaking his head. "When did he disappear?"

"Sometime around 8:30 this morning, a Super Cleaners van taken from Evergreen Hills showed up at his house and apparently was used to abduct him," Brigid explained.

"Evergreen Hills, huh?" Luis asked. "That makes sense."

"Why is that?" Brigid asked.

"Jesse has the manager for Super Cleaners in Evergreen Hills under his thumb. I'm not entirely sure what he has on the guy, but when he tells the man to jump, he does. My guess would be the guy owes him money."

Luis shook his head. "If he did this himself or sent someone else, that means Jesse was getting impatient. At this point, I'm not even sure what that would mean. For him not to wait around or let me know what was going on, can't be good."

"Right now all we're working with is speculation," Deputy Keegan said. "But if you have any ideas where he may have taken Mike, it sure would help us. Maybe a place where he likes to hide things, since you said he doesn't usually do stuff like this."

Luis thought for a moment. "He has various properties, but I have a couple of ideas. One is much more likely than the others. It's a small older warehouse on the edge of town. There's not a lot of development out there. I remember the reason he bought it was because it was dirt cheap. The owner just wanted to get rid of it, and Jesse thought it could end up being useful in his operations. To my knowledge he only uses it for storage, but he could have taken Mike there. Seems like something he'd do."

"Here's what I'm thinking," Detective Baptiste interjected. "What if we do a sort of small-time sting? You call Jesse and make sure that's where he is. Then, get him to invite you there. When you go, you wear a wire and get him to admit to some of his crimes. You find out where Mike is, we get plenty of dirt to bury Jesse for a long, long time, and you get to move on with your life." The detective sat back and steepled his fingers. "What do you think?"

"But what if he isn't there? Or he doesn't want me to come to wherever he is?" Luis asked, worried.

"I'm sure you can think of something," Detective Baptiste said.

"Maybe," Luis said carefully. "But I can't make any promises."

"Why don't you just try?" Brigid asked. "You won't know unless you do, and I'm worried that the longer we wait, the less time Mike Loomis may have to live."

"Okay, I'll give it a shot," Luis said, nodding. He pulled out his cell phone. "But you guys can't make a sound. Even if he had me followed, I rode my motorcycle, and went places no tail could go, so I'm sure he doesn't know I'm here. If he so much as thinks there's someone in the room with me, it could be all over before it even begins."

Everyone was silent as he scrolled through his phone and found Jesse's contact information. Once he pushed the button, he put it up to his ear.

"Hey, Jesse. How's it going, man?" he asked casually. "That's good. I'm calling because I really need to talk to you in person. You know I'm not a fan of talking business on the phone. No, don't worry about it. I can come to you."

He looked up and nodded to everyone else. Brigid took that to mean Jesse had taken the bait. "Okay, I'll get there as soon as I can. See you in a few." He ended his call and turned off his phone. "He's at the warehouse, just like I thought."

"Great," Detective Baptiste said with a grin. "I know of the perfect vehicle for us to take. We have an undercover vehicle we can use so we can listen in and record your conversation."

He looked as though he was a cat who had just cornered a mouse. "Let me go talk to some people, and we'll be ready to go in a few minutes. It shouldn't take long." He stood up and left the room, leaving the rest of them sitting anxiously.

"Luis, how do we know you didn't take Mike Loomis and you're letting your boss take the fall?" Deputy Keegan finally asked.

"You'll know different once you hear it through the wire," Luis said as he leaned back in his chair. "But I don't blame you for being wary. You should be. As far as you know, I'm the bad guy."

"Why now?" Sheriff Davis interrupted. "Why sell your boss out now? I get it that he asked ya' to cross a line, but still. Why didn't ya' jes' do the job and be done with it. You'd probably end up better off than by turnin' him in."

"It does sound crazy, doesn't it?" Luis admitted. "But the thing is, Jesse isn't like your average man. He's let his power and influence go to his head. Sure, I could have taken care of Mike for him, and he would have made sure my family wanted for nothing.

"But I know him. He'd dangle it over my head whenever he decided he needed another favor. I wouldn't put it past him to try and extend his influence to wherever I moved. With men like Jesse, you aren't ever truly free of them. They pull you in with expensive things and nice houses, but they know they can jerk them out from under you whenever they feel like it."

"So why turn him in?" Brigid asked. "Wouldn't his other guys find out and come after you?"

"Detective Baptiste and I have a plan for that," he explained. "The main point is that we make it look like I'm getting arrested right along with him. Then my family and I get relocated somewhere far away from here."

The door opened and the detective stepped inside. "It's ready and waiting outside. Are you guys ready?"

As they followed Detective Baptiste out of the room, Brigid was surprised at how her day was turning out. She'd had no clue when she'd gotten up that morning that she'd be in Denver by the end of the day helping catch a guy who sounded like something on a TV program, a big-time crime boss in the making. She pulled out her phone and sent Linc yet another text to let him know she'd probably be late.

She'd texted him earlier, telling him that she was going to Denver with the sheriff on a case. Slipping her phone back into her purse, she was grateful for her gun. If this guy was as bad as he sounded, she didn't want to take any more risks than she had to. She had every intention of making it home to sleep peacefully next to her husband tonight.

Detective Baptiste led them outside and Brigid had to blink at the brightness. When she could finally open her eyes, she was a little surprised at what was in front of them.

"Here she is," the detective said sounding as if he was a proud father. "Our transportation."

In front of them was an older RV that was covered in dirt and looked as though it had definitely seen better days.

"Are you serious?" Deputy Keegan asked.

"Sure am. Nobody would ever suspect this vehicle of being part of law enforcement," he said with a grin.

"No, but they sure might think it's a meth lab," Deputy Keegan said as she leaned toward Brigid who snickered. She was right, it looked like something that would be on a TV show.

"That's smart," Luis said with a satisfactory nod.

"Don't worry, it's been upgraded inside. Let's go, time's a-wasting," the detective said as he opened the door. "Climb aboard."

CHAPTER NINETEEN

"This should be as good a place as any to sit and listen," Detective Baptiste said as he pulled in behind a high dense hedge located about fifty feet from the warehouse building.

They were in an area that looked as though it was an abandoned industrial zone. Older factories and buildings were vacant, and grass was growing up between the cracks in the parking lots. Brigid thought the area had a spooky feeling to it, and she wouldn't have been surprised to see a tumbleweed or shambling zombie come around a corner.

Detective Baptiste made his way to the back of the RV and began opening drawers. "Let's get you wired up Luis, so you can head inside." The detective made quick work of setting up the hidden microphone and then checking to make sure it would transmit. "We're parked close enough that we should hear you with absolutely no trouble, no matter where you go inside the building. This thing has some serious range on it, and it's designed to go through concrete walls."

"Good, I wouldn't want to go through all of this for nothing," Luis chuckled nervously.

"We'll be in here, listenin'. We got yer' back," Sheriff Davis said with a nod. "Yer' on our side now. Just do like we was discussin' on the way over here, and it should all go off without a hitch."

"I will," Luis said. "I just hope he's not done something stupid." He shook his head and sighed. "Am I ready?"

"Yep, whenever you feel up to it, everything is a go," Detective Baptiste said.

Luis stood up and went to the door on the side of the RV. "Here goes nothing. Wish me luck." Flipping the door open, he stepped out into the early evening.

While they waited for Luis to get to the building, Brigid looked around the RV. It wasn't huge, but it wasn't the smallest one she'd ever seen, either. For the most part, you could still tell what it once had been, but there were various types of equipment that had been installed in places that used to have cabinets and drawers. She and Deputy Keegan were seated at the table area while Sheriff Davis and Detective Baptiste sat near the equipment, ready to listen in.

"I'm just walking into the building," they heard Luis whisper.

Brigid felt as though her heart would beat right out of her chest. She knew she was perfectly safe in the RV, but she was terrified for Luis. Knowing he had a family back home made her feel even more for him.

Granted, he'd probably done some bad things working for Jesse, but the fact that he knew right from wrong made her feel a great deal of compassion towards him. He was refusing to murder someone, even though he and his family could have all they wanted if he did. How many other people would do that, given the situation?

The sound of a door squeaking came through the speaker and then Luis called, "Jesse? Where are you, man?"

Brigid could almost envision the entire thing as if it was happening in front of her. She imagined that the building was dark on the inside, the only light coming in the high windows, which were broken and dirty.

"Over here," they heard a voice say. It sounded distant and faint. "Behind the container."

Footsteps echoed and pretty soon Luis said, "Man, this place is really out here, huh? I don't think I've ever been here. I remember you telling me about it though."

"It's a pretty good place, isn't it?" Jesse said. "I've been doing a lot of thinking while I've been here today. I need to utilize this space more. I mean, it's perfect for just about anything."

"That it is," Luis agreed. "You could probably let the nature stuff grow up around the outside to give it some privacy."

"I could," Jesse said. Brigid could imagine the man nodding. She'd only seen pictures of him on Deputy Keegan's computer, but she could still envision him.

"Come on, get what we need," Detective Baptiste muttered.

"Give him time," Sheriff Davis said. "He can't exactly jes' bring it up outta' nowhere."

"Shh, we can't hear," Deputy Keegan interrupted.

"This sort of space would have been great when you got that big shipment," Luis was saying. "Remember how you brought all that stuff in and you had to store it in those little storage lockers?"

"Oh, are you talking about that time when I accidentally ordered twice the product?" Jesse chuckled. "That was a mess, but it all worked out."

"You've definitely had some close calls over the years," Luis began. "Like that time when you set fire to that guy's business. Who was that again?"

"You mean Marshall? The guy with the restaurant that used to be next door to the club? Yeah, I was a little nervous about that one. But I must have done something right because the cops seemed to have dropped the case," Jesse said confidently.

"How did you do that, anyway?" Luis asked. "I don't think you ever told me."

"It was fairly simple. They used gas stoves, so I just turned on all of the burners and tossed some cleaning towels on them. He was even dumb enough to tell me he didn't have a security system when I first started the club. That's how I knew I could get away with it. No proof, no conviction. But I tried to reason with him. I offered him a fair price for everything, but he wouldn't budge. Once the place burned, I got it all for a fraction of the price."

"He really didn't know who he was messing with, did he?" Luis said with a chuckle.

"No, he didn't," Jesse said. "Kind of like that guy after that kid overdosed. He kept yelling and screaming, making a scene. Blaming me for his kid's death or whatever. Like I made her buy my coke and put it up her nose. You remember her?"

"I think so, but refresh my memory," Luis said.

"You don't remember that girl? She bought coke from me in the club and then went in the bathroom. We had to dump her body somewhere else so we wouldn't get busted for selling out of the club. Besides, death is bad for business," Jesse tsked. "Which brings me to what I've been doing today."

"Yeah, so what are you doing here?" Luis asked.

"Well, I had half of my shipment delivered here today, and the rest should be coming once it's dark. But I decided I needed to get involved in that little project I wanted you to do," he said.

"You mean the guy who used to work for us?" Luis asked.

"Exactly. I know you said you were working on it and all, but I had a brilliant idea. So, I took a little road trip myself. I have Mike Loomis here." The way he said those words so calmly chilled Brigid to the bone. Who could talk about these horrible things like that? As if they were describing a family picnic or an evening out on the town.

"What do you mean, you have him here? Did you kill him? How did you do it?" Luis asked, surprised.

"No, I haven't killed him. I was waiting for you so you can uphold your end of the deal. But I didn't want him talking to the cops any more than he already had, so I drove over to Evergreen Hills where I have that guy who runs a Super Cleaners under my thumb. Told him I'd need a van and not to ask questions.

"Drove it over to Cottonwood Springs and pretended I was a cleaning crew when I went there. The guy had left his door partially open, so I just walked right on in. He put up a fight, but I knocked him out and threw him in the van."

"Now what?" Luis asked.

"Now we deal with him just like we'd deal with anyone who stands in my way," Jesse responded.

"But what if the guy didn't tell anyone anything?" Luis asked. "What if he didn't do anything wrong?"

"Are you getting soft, Luis? I'm not worried about right or wrong. I'm worried about an ex druggie standing in my way. He's an obstacle and needs to be removed. Just like the restaurant, the overdose girl, all those people I've had you rough up over the years. I need him dead and gone, so that I can rest at night." They could tell that Jesse was getting agitated.

"I hear you. Just like all those businesses that you would have someone break into only to offer them protection," Luis supplied.

"Yeah, something like that," he said. "There are two types of people in the world, Luis, the wolves and the sheep. If you don't have the guts to act like a wolf, then you're no better than a sheep."

"Hey, I can act like a wolf," Luis said, indignantly. "I just don't know if you should be bringing heat on yourself like this. Killing a man for no reason could backfire."

"I have a reason, to protect my empire," Jesse said simply. "I've worked far too hard to have it all taken away by some ex druggie who decided to come clean. It's not like he's a pillar of society, Luis. The man has done his fair share of bad. Let God decide his punishment. You're simply freeing him before he goes back to the drugs and does it himself."

"I guess that makes sense," Luis said. "Where is he?"

"He's in that room over there on the far left," Jesse said.

"You mean the only one that's painted red?" Luis asked.

"That's the one, come on," Jesse said. "Better to just get it over with."

"We better go in," Sheriff Davis said. "It's gone far enough."

"He hasn't gotten much out of him yet," Detective Baptiste objected. "I want more to make sure I put this low-life away for life."

"That should be enough," Sheriff Davis said. "We gotta' get in there."

"No, just a little longer," the detective said.

Sheriff Davis made an indignant noise. "Ya' hide in here if ya' wanna'. I'm goin' in." He stood up and hurried out of the RV.

Deputy Keegan shimmed out of her seat and rushed after him.

"Guess you guys do things a little different here," Brigid said quickly as she pulled out her gun and followed her friends.

CHAPTER TWENTY

"Wait, I've got backup coming," Detective Baptiste called out as she shut the door behind her. Brigid didn't know how the detective was used to doing things, but she and the Sheriff always had each other's back. It seemed as though Deputy Keegan was the same way. She was close behind the sheriff when Brigid caught up to them.

"We'll go in the same door that Luis went in," Sheriff Davis instructed. "Brigid, ya' hang back a bit. We both got vests on, so we're more equipped if this turns ugly."

Brigid nodded. "Will do."

Silently, they slipped up beside the one-story concrete building. It reminded Brigid of those older airline hangar style buildings, the ones where the windows were much higher than on regular buildings, but there were large doors on either end. If this building had ever held a plane, it would have had to have been a small two-seater.

Sheriff Davis carefully pulled the door open and peeked around the corner before slipping inside. Brigid knew she'd done some questionable things in her life, but this was probably at the top of the list. If Holly and Linc knew what she was doing, she knew they'd be screaming at her to run back to the RV.

But she knew there was no way she could do that. She may not have the years of training that the sheriff and deputy had received, but that didn't mean she couldn't be useful. What if they got into a situation where they needed her help? She'd never be able to forgive herself for not being there for them.

Just as she'd imagined, it was dark inside. There were a couple of dim lights in the distance that cast long shadows on things, making it hard to tell what they were. She saw a metal shipping container, something that looked a bit like a boiler or something similar, and a couple of crates in the large room. There were doors in the distance, and she spotted one that was painted red.

Sheriff Davis pointed toward that door and both women nodded. They hurried towards the wall and silently crept along it, doing their best to listen. Brigid could hear what she thought may have been the sounds of muffled talking, but she wasn't certain. It might have just been strange sounds that the building made.

Brigid was sure everyone could hear the blood rushing through her veins and the pounding of her heart. She didn't want to focus too much on how sweaty her palms were or how much her hands were shaking. She kept her training in the forefront of her mind. She'd prepared for this, and she knew it.

The door squeaked open, and Jesse stepped out into the darkness. They were out of his line of sight for a moment, but Brigid caught the glint of a pistol in his hand.

"I'll be right back," he was saying. "Then, we'll get this taken care of." As he turned to look back in the illuminated room, he caught sight of them. "Hey," he shouted as he lifted his gun and fired a shot in their direction.

Deputy Keegan pushed Brigid behind a stack of crates in the dark as she and Sheriff Davis returned fire.

"Freeze," Sheriff Davis yelled. He shouted a few more things, but Brigid couldn't hear what he said. The sound of gunshots echoed throughout the cavernous space of the building.

Brigid peeked around the corner of the crate she was hiding behind and saw Sheriff Davis and Deputy Keegan hiding behind some other crates. As she leaned a little farther out, she saw Jesse next to the shipping container. He was focused on Davis and Keegan, apparently unaware that she was there.

"Luis, where in the devil are you?" he yelled.

"I don't have a gun, Jesse," Luis said in a loud voice from inside the room.

"You're worthless," Jesse muttered. "You know that?" he yelled. "You're worthless. If you would have just done as you were told…" he stopped speaking long enough to fire another shot in the sheriff's direction.

Deputy Keegan looked over at Brigid and signaled for her to stay low. Brigid shook her head and pantomimed that she could see Jesse. Keegan shook her head and once again signaled for her to stay down.

But I have a shot, Brigid thought. Just then, Sheriff Davis poked out from his hiding spot and took a shot, narrowly missing Jesse.

"Might as well give yerself' up," Sheriff Davis called out. "Got backup waitin' jes' outside. Ya' got nowhere to go, and there ain't enough places to hide in here."

"That's where you're wrong," Jesse yelled back. "You have no idea what I'm capable of, and I know it's just you two. Your uniforms don't look like Denver officers, so I'm willing to bet you're some small-time cops who thought you'd land a big fish. But let me tell you, you're out of your depth. I'm not a fish, I'm a shark."

Brigid could faintly hear sirens in the distance.

"That don't sound like we're alone to me," Sheriff Davis said in a loud voice. Brigid couldn't take it. If the sheriff stuck his head out at the wrong time, nothing would save him. The same went for Deputy Keegan. Brigid turned and looked the other way, back towards the door Jesse had come out of. Luis was peering out and caught sight of her. He was behind Jesse, so Jesse couldn't see that the person he thought was his partner was trying to signal to someone.

"I'll distract him," Luis mouthed to her. "You shoot."

Brigid bit her lip. Shooting a pistol at target practice was one thing, but she wasn't sure if she could pull the trigger while she aimed it at another human being. Could she take this man's life if she had to? Instantly, she regretted even thinking it. It wasn't like she had a choice. She didn't have the option to pick and choose right now.

There was a bad man who had already admitted to doing some very bad things trying to shoot her friends. This wasn't something that was up for debate. He'd taken the choice away from her when he decided to open fire on them. Thankfully, Deputy Keegan had been thinking when she'd shoved Brigid behind a crate. It gave them an advantage. She knew that wasn't what Lindsey had anticipated when she'd pushed her. She'd only wanted to keep Brigid safe. But wasn't that what Brigid was doing? Keeping her friends safe?

She recalled a time from her training when she'd practiced shooting for the first time with the sheriff.

"I will do absolutely everythin' in my power to make sure ya' don't ever have to use this," he'd promised her as he'd held out the gun. "But I know that yer' safer if ya' got a means to protect yerself'. In our line of work, ya' never know when the simplest case could turn into somethin' far bigger than we anticipate.

"I'll always do what I can to protect ya', and so will my deputies, but there may come a time when ya' need to use these skills. I want ya' to practice and hone them 'til ya' feel confident enough to do it in yer' sleep. That's the only way I'm gonna' feel comfortable enough takin' ya' in the field with me."

Brigid had taken the gun from him that day, never truly expecting to have to fire it at a person. But here she was, and they needed her. Sheriff Davis may not have anticipated needing her to back him up, but that was the reason she'd followed them out of the RV. It had been a hunch or instinct that had told her to get up and follow them. Now she knew why. Because if she hadn't, they wouldn't have anyone to help them.

She peeked back around at Luis and nodded her head. She was ready. This was her time to make a move. No hesitation. Just pure analytical thinking as she'd been taught. She watched as Luis tossed a glass bottle from the room, causing it to shatter behind Jesse. He whirled around, looking for the source of the sound.

Brigid stood up from behind the crate, gun raised. She only took a moment to aim at Jesse. She set her sights on his shoulder and squeezed the trigger. The power of the gun jumping in her hand and the loud bang made her ears ring. It almost sounded like a second shot was fired and then another. She watched as Jesse crumpled to the floor.

"Are you okay?" Deputy Keegan cried out as she ran over to Brigid.

Brigid nodded, still in shock. That was when she felt pain begin to radiate on the left side of her body. She couldn't quite pinpoint where. Maybe her shoulder? She lifted her hand to where she thought the pain was coming from and touched it gingerly. The intensity increased, and her vision began to get fuzzy as the ringing in her ears grew louder. When she pulled her hand away, it felt sticky and was red with blood.

"Oh my God, Brigid," Deputy Keegan gasped. "You've been shot. You're going to be okay. Just stay with me." She wrapped her arms around Brigid as Brigid began to lose her vision. Everything went black as she fainted into her friend's arms.

CHAPTER TWENTY-ONE

When Brigid came to, she was lying on an ambulance type of gurney.

"Oh, thank God you're awake," Deputy Keegan gasped. "You scared the life out of me."

"What happened?" Brigid asked as she looked around. It was almost completely dark, yet the area was lit up with blue and red strobes as well as bright flood lights.

"Ya' passed out," Sheriff Davis said as he came up behind Lindsey. "Scared the holy hell out of both of us, but yer' gonn' be okay."

"Sometimes I get kinda woozy when I see blood," Brigid admitted. "It's a thing of mine that I've had since I was a little girl." She still felt a little out of it and was having trouble putting her thoughts together. It was as if she'd woken up from a deep sleep.

"Good to know," Deputy Keegan said as she rolled her eyes.

Brigid finally became aware that an EMT was standing beside her. He'd been there the whole time but she hadn't noticed.

"You were shot, but it just grazed you. I got you all stitched up and you're as good as new," the EMT said. "Just relax for now.

Here's a bottle of water if you're thirsty." He turned and walked away as she sat up.

"Did we get him?" Brigid asked.

"We did," Sheriff Davis said. "Ya' shot him in the shoulder, and I got him in the leg. He's under arrest and headed to the hospital."

"Good," Brigid said, as she began to focus on her surroundings. "How's Mike?"

"It appears that Jesse beat on him a bit, but he'll survive," Deputy Keegan said. "He went to the hospital and Luis was taken to the station."

Brigid gingerly turned to the side of the gurney and lowered her feet to the ground.

"Take it easy there, champ. Don't need ya' passin' out again," Sheriff Davis said with a chuckle.

"I'll be fine," Brigid reassured them. "I'm already feeling better."

"Good, because we got a long drive home ahead of us," Sheriff Davis said.

"Speaking of," Brigid began. "What were you going to tell us about Detective Baptiste?" she asked Deputy Keegan.

"Oh, that?" she said as she looked away. "It's really not important. Before I left the department, he kept trying to get me to go out on a date with him. Apparently one time he'd told some of the guys at the station that he was going out with me, but I shot him down. He didn't tell them that, though.

"He went on to make them believe we'd gone out and had a great time, even going back to his place afterwards. I called him out on it, but he denied it. Shortly after that I transferred to Cottonwood Springs."

"What a jerk," Brigid said shaking her head. "Guys like that get on my nerves."

"Oh girl, how I know," Sheriff Davis said in his best girl impression. Both Brigid and Lindsey laughed.

"Looks like you're feeling better," the EMT said as he returned. "I'd say you're good to go. Just follow up with your doctor."

"I will," Brigid promised.

*****

It took about two hours to drive back to Cottonwood Springs from Denver. As they approached Brigid's home, Sheriff Davis said, "Ya' make sure Linc and Holly take good care of ya', hear?"

"I will," Brigid said. "I'll say it's by orders of the sheriff."

"Sounds right," he said with a nod. "Don't know about you ladies, but I feel like I could stay up all night after all that excitement."

"Not me," Brigid said. "I'm exhausted."

"I won't be able to sleep," Deputy Keegan said as she shook her head. "It's going to be a long night. I'll probably make a pizza."

"Man, that sounds good," Sheriff Davis muttered. "I wish somethin' was still open, I'd grab one."

"I have more than enough. You're welcome to share some of mine," she said quickly.

Brigid smiled to herself in the back seat. She hadn't thought about it before, but Sheriff Davis and Deputy Keegan would make a nice couple. Plus, they seemed to get along well. As they pulled up in front of her house, she carefully undid her seat belt.

"Ya' sure you don't need help?" Sheriff Davis asked.

"No, I've got it. Thank you. You two enjoy your night," she said as she climbed out of the back. They waited for her to get to her porch before pulling away into the night.

Twisting the door knob, she stepped into the house, grateful to be home.

"Thank goodness you're home," Linc said as he stood up from his chair and rushed to her. Jett and Lucky came trotting over to her with Holly right behind them.

"I'm okay, really," she said for what felt like the millionth time. She'd already told Linc on the phone she was okay.

"Still, you were hurt," Linc said.

"You were shot!" Holly pointed out. "We're going to baby you, okay?"

"Okay," Brigid said. "But do I get bonus points for taking down the bad guy?"

"I guess so," Linc said. "But I'd rather you didn't do that sort of thing anymore. Chasing after big time bad guys, I mean."

"Are you kidding?" Holly asked. "How much you want to bet she ends up on the news?"

"I don't know about that," Brigid said bashfully. The clock over the fireplace began to chime, letting her know it was late.

"Come on, let's get everyone to bed. We can talk about all this in the morning," Brigid said as she ushered everyone away from the front door.

"But there's no way I can sleep now," Holly whined.

"You'll just have to find a way," Brigid said. "I need a good night's rest, and I can't get that staying up all night talking to you. I'll give you all the details in the morning at breakfast. I even read about a breakfast pizza I'm going to make for you."

"All right," Holly grumbled. "At least I'll have something to look forward to. Come on Lucky. Let's go to bed." She carefully gave Brigid a hug and then hugged Linc before heading to her room and shutting the door.

"So it just grazed you, huh?" Linc asked as he followed her to their bedroom.

"That's what the paramedic told me," Brigid said as she walked over to the closet. Linc shut the door behind them.

"Let me see," he said as he moved toward her. He helped her lift her shirt over her head and then pulled the bandage back.

"He said there were seven stitches," she said as she got her first look at it herself. It didn't look nearly as bad as she'd imagined.

"Lucky number seven, hmm?" Linc said as he carefully replaced the bandage. "You really gave me a scare, Brigid."

"I know, and I'm sorry. But things could have been so much worse if I wasn't there. You just don't understand," she said shaking her head. "It was a bad situation, sure, but if I'd stayed behind in the RV, I don't know what would have happened to the sheriff or Deputy Keegan."

"Well then, I guess it was a good thing you were there," he said. "And that the other guy was such a bad shot. It could have been just a little farther this way," he said as he slowly dragged his finger across her collar bone.

"Trust me, I know. Plus, I think I shaved a few years off of Sheriff Davis' life when I passed out," Brigid chuckled.

"You really aren't that great with blood, are you?" he asked with a grin.

"It's kind of strange," Brigid admitted. "Small amounts, no problem. Large amounts don't seem to be a problem either. But there is a point in the middle that just bothers me."

Linc shrugged. "You're weird."

"Thanks," Brigid scoffed as she worked to finish changing into a nightgown.

"Here, let me help," Linc said. "You need to take it easy for a while."

"That's what the sheriff said," she said with a yawn.

"Come on, let's get in bed so I can hold you and be grateful I have you in my life," Linc said as he tugged his own shirt off.

"Now that sounds like a plan," Brigid said as she pulled the blankets back and climbed into bed. The cool sheets felt inviting as she twisted onto her side, bad shoulder up. Linc snuggled up behind her, wrapping his arm around her waist. Within minutes she was sound asleep.

EPILOGUE

A few days later Brigid pulled in her driveway to find a sheriff's department car parked outside. She was mildly curious as to what was going on. She climbed out of her car and walked up to the house, wondering if they had another case to work on and the sheriff had come by hoping to catch her at home.

She pulled out her phone as she climbed the steps to the porch, checking to see if she had any messages from Sheriff Davis, but didn't find any. She twisted the doorknob and stepped inside.

"Hey, Brigid," Sheriff Davis said with a smile. Deputy Keegan was sitting beside him on the couch.

"What are you guys doing here?" Brigid asked. "Is something wrong?"

"Not at all," Deputy Keegan said. "We just wanted to stop by and tell you what we heard."

"Oh, okay," Brigid said as she set her purse down and pulled off her jacket. Jett was at her feet, bumping into her legs, and demanding attention. "Hang on big guy," she said with a chuckle. "Let me sit down first." He followed her as she went over to a chair and took a seat, plopping down right in front of her.

"We've kept the media away from the story 'bout Jesse Stanford as long as possible," Sheriff Davis began. "But they'll be runnin' it purty soon. They want to interview everyone involved. I'm leaving it up to ya' if ya' want to be recognized."

"You can do that?" Brigid asked.

"I can do whatever I want when it comes to somethin' like this. I know ya' like to keep to yerself', Brigid. If ya' don't want to talk to 'em, I'll tell 'em that. Maintain anonymity and all of that," he said. "It's not like yer' officially an officer, although if ya' were, I'd be proud to have ya'."

"I don't really know if I want to talk about it," Brigid admitted. "But at the same time, I don't want to feel like I'm hiding."

"Well, you have a day or so to decide," Deputy Keegan explained. "You might want to think about it, though. It doesn't matter to us, but you helped take down a pretty big criminal. We don't know if there will be people who are angry and want revenge. With you having a family and all of that..." she shrugged and let her sentence trail off.

"Let me think about it," Brigid said with a nod. "What happened with Luis?"

"From what I've heard, he's been extremely cooperative with the Denver police and has helped them immensely in building their case against Jesse Stanford. Last I heard, he's planning on taking his family to Alaska when it's over," Sheriff Davis said.

"Wow, that's quite a move," Linc said. He'd moved from his chair to stand beside Brigid and was gently rubbing her shoulders. She smiled as she looked at him, knowing that the reason he'd been so hands-on with her lately was because of her getting shot. Even if it was just a graze, it seemed to have made him acutely aware of her mortality. But Brigid didn't mind the attention. She intended to soak it up while she could.

"Derek Walden is awaiting trial," Deputy Keegan said. "He had a lot more drugs in his car and at his house. I don't think he'll be getting out early like Mike Loomis did."

"Good riddance then," Brigid said as she continued to scratch Jett behind his ears. "We don't need that stuff around here."

"Hopefully it sends a message, at least fer a little while, that sellin' drugs in Cottonwood Springs will only get ya' arrested," Sheriff Davis said proudly. "I'd much rather spend my time sittin' in my car checkin' fer speeders."

"In other news," Brigid began, "Linc is getting ready to break ground over at his house next door. We're adding on so we can turn it into a B & B." She was so glad she'd said yes and allowed Linc to do what he wanted. He seemed to love the planning and preparation. He'd been talking about it nonstop since she'd gotten home from Denver.

"That's great, when do you think construction will start?" Deputy Keegan asked.

"As a matter of fact, today they start working on the foundation and some grading to level things out," Linc said proudly. "I need to get over there," he said looking at his watch. "They should be here soon."

"Ya' mind showin' me what yer' buildin'?" Sheriff Davis asked.

"Not at all," Linc said eagerly. "You two want to come?" He looked at Brigid and Deputy Keegan who shook their heads.

"I'm not any good at seeing stuff in my head. But once it gets going, I'll definitely stop by and take a look," Lindsay said. She and Sheriff Davis exchanged a glance that seemed like something more to Brigid.

Waiting until the men had left, she turned to Lindsey and said, "That was some look you two just exchanged."

"What do you mean?" Deputy Keegan asked innocently.

"Oh, I know a look when I see one," Brigid said with a smile. "Is something going on between you two?"

"Is it that obvious?" Deputy Keegan gasped.

"No, not at all," Brigid reassured. "I just have an eye for that sort of thing."

"We don't really have anything going on right now," she admitted. "But there's chemistry. The other night, after we dropped you off? Nothing happened, but you could feel it in the air, you know? Like static electricity or something. There were all these meaningful looks and small touches. But he seems like he's trying to keep his distance."

"Maybe he is," Brigid shrugged. "I mean, technically he's your boss. There could be all sorts of things that could get in the way. Plus, other people in the department might feel like you could get preferential treatment if you two were dating."

"I don't think he'd do that," Lindsey said as she looked toward the door.

"I don't think so either," Brigid said gently. "But he doesn't have to do anything for people to accuse him of it. You know that. I bet he's just trying to be professional. Have you said anything?"

Deputy Keegan shook her head. "No, I've been too nervous to. I wasn't sure if he was even interested."

"I definitely think he is," Brigid assured her. "Just take it slow. I think he needs a little time. That's all."

Deputy Keegan nodded. "I will. And who knows, maybe it was all just because we went through that ordeal in Denver together. You know how something like that goes."

"I do," Brigid said. "And it could be. But I don't really think that's it. Either way, let me know what happens."

"I will," Deputy Keegan said with a grin. "I think you're the only person I'd be able to talk to about it."

"I'm always around," Brigid replied. "Just a phone call away."

*****

Brigid and Linc stood nearby as they watched the workmen pouring concrete for the foundation. Linc couldn't help it, he was grinning like crazy as he watched his new project begin.

"This is going to be great," he said for the fifth time since Brigid had come over to watch.

"So you've said," she said with a sly nudge.

"I'm sorry," Linc said with the shake of his head. "I don't mean to sound like a broken record."

"No, it's fine," she said as she slipped her arm around him. "I know you're excited. It's good you're this happy about it. I hope it all turns out just as you imagine."

"It will. I know it." He pulled her close and kissed her temple. "I keep thinking about all the interesting people we'll meet and the time we'll spend with strangers who will hopefully become friends."

"I doubt if you're going to make friends with everyone who stays here," Brigid said doubtfully.

"Challenge accepted," he said happily. "I love you, Brigid."

"I love you too, Linc." Brigid could feel her love for him expanding in her chest like a balloon.

"Got any ideas what we should call this new place of ours?" Linc asked. "I'm going to have to start filling out paperwork and such, so

142

we're going to need a name for it."

"You know, I hadn't really thought about that," Brigid admitted. "I don't know why."

"Well, you have been busy with your own stuff. But I do want this to be ours, so I'd like your input for the name," Linc said gently.

"Have you come up with anything?" Brigid asked.

"I had a couple I thought about, but none of them felt like the right one," he admitted.

"Tell me what they were, so I have an idea of where you're going with this," Brigid said.

"Well, I did some research, and the articles I read said it's best to not use your name in case you ever want to sell it. It said it's best to pick something marketable. I'd thought something like 'Black Dog Inn' or something silly like 'Pull Inn.' But neither one of those are it."

"No," Brigid said. "You're right. They're cute, but I don't feel anything from them. Maybe you need to think about what this Bed and Breakfast will be to you," she suggested. "How does it make you feel when you think about it?"

"It's hard to explain," Linc sighed. He continued to watch the men work as he thought. "I feel like this is all a new beginning. Slowing down and being a family. Welcoming people into our place with open arms, it's like the dawn of a new life when I see all of this and think about where it's going."

"So, why not something like 'New Dawn Inn?'" she asked. "Then you could make the logo look like a rising sun or something like that."

"Brigid, you're a genius," Linc said as a smile spread across his face. "That's perfect."

"Really?" Brigid asked. "Are you sure?"

"Don't you like it?" Linc asked, suddenly worried.

"Of course I like it, but you don't have to pick it. I was just thinking out loud," she said shaking her head.

"No, it's perfect," he said as he turned toward her. "Welcome to the New Dawn Inn."

RECIPES

PEANUT BUTTER BANANA SMOOTHIE

Ingredients:
2 bananas, peeled and broken into chunks
2 cups milk
½ cup smooth peanut butter
3 tbsp. honey
2 cups ice cubes, crushed

Directions:
Place the ingredients in a blender. Blend until smooth, about 30 seconds. Pour into glasses and enjoy!

CROCK POT CHICKEN AND DUMPLINGS

Ingredients:
1 onion, roughly chopped
1 ¼ lb. boneless skinless chicken breasts
1 tsp. dried oregano
Kosher salt to taste
Freshly ground pepper to taste
2 cups chicken broth (I prefer Better Than Bouillon.)
3 cans (10.5 oz.) cream of chicken soup

4 springs fresh thyme
1 bay leaf
2 stalks celery, chopped
2 carrots, peeled and chopped (I often don't peel them.)
1 cup frozen peas, thawed
3 garlic cloves, minced
½ (16.3 oz.) can refrigerated biscuits

Directions:
Scatter onions in the bottom of a large slow cooker then top with chicken. Season with oregano, salt, and pepper. Pour the soup and broth over the mixture and add the thyme and bay leaf. Cover and cook on high until the chicken is cooked, about 3 hours.

Discard the thyme and bay leaf. Shred chicken with two forks. Stir in celery, carrots, peas, and garlic. Cut biscuits into small pieces and stir into chicken mixture. Spoon a little liquid over biscuits. Cook on high until vegetables are tender and biscuits are cooked through, about 1 hour more. Enjoy!

NOTE: I found the biscuits browned better if I put the mixture in a 425 degree over for the last 30 minutes

Mushroom Caps with Wine Sauce

Ingredients:
1 lb. baby Bella mushrooms (about 12-14)
2 tbsp. unsalted butter
1 tbsp. olive oil
4 garlic cloves, finely minced
2 tbsp. shallots, finely minced (You can substitute white onion.)
½ cup Worcestershire sauce
½ cup red wine
½ tsp. cornstarch
1 tbsp. water

Directions:

Rinse mushrooms, leaving stems on. Pat dry with paper towel. In a heavy-duty frying pan, heat butter and olive oil until foaming. Add garlic and shallots. Sauté 2-3 minutes over medium-high heat.

Add mushrooms, Worcestershire sauce, and red wine. Cook over medium-low heat, turning occasionally, until mushrooms turn brown and liquid is reduced by half (about 7-8 minutes). Mix cornstarch with water to make a slurry and slowly add it to the mushroom mixture until it reaches your desired thickness. Serve and enjoy!

MINI BREAKFAST PIZZAS

Ingredients:

2 cups granola (without flax seeds)
¼ cup unsalted butter, melted
2 tbsp. honey
2 containers vanilla yogurt (5 oz. each)
1 cup mixed berries (your choice)
2 tbsp. creamy peanut butter
1 tbsp. cooking oil
2 tbsp. toasted sliced almonds.

Directions:

Preheat oven to 350 degrees. Add granola to food processor and process 8 seconds until coarsely ground. Transfer to medium size bowl. Add butter and honey, combine. Divide & form into 4 rounds, 4" in diameter and ½" thick. Form the rounds by patting them with your fingers until rounded equally. Place on cookie sheet and bake 8-9 minutes until lightly brown at edges. Cool completely or bake ahead of time.

To serve: Top each granola round with yogurt. Sprinkle berries on top. Mix peanut butter and oil. Heat in microwave for 15 seconds to warm. Drizzle peanut butter on top. Garnish with almonds. Serve and enjoy!

Banana Split Pie

Ingredients:
Crust:
5 cups crushed vanilla wafers (about 2 boxes)
6 tbsp. unsalted butter, melted
½ cup sugar

Filling:
4 ripe bananas, peeled and sliced ½" thick
1 pint vanilla ice cream, softened
1 pint chocolate ice cream, softened
1 pint strawberry ice cream, softened
1 16 oz. jar Hot Fudge Chocolate Sauce

Topping:
2 cups heavy cream
2 tbsp. sifted powdered sugar
1 cup chopped dry-roasted peanuts

Directions:
Preheat oven to 325 degrees. Coat two 9" pie pans with nonstick cooking spray. In a large bowl, stir together the crumbs, melted butter, and sugar until well-combined. Press into prepared pie pans and bake until crust begins to crisp, 6-8 minutes. Remove from oven and cool completely.

To make the filling, cover the bottom of the crust with a layer of sliced bananas. Place alternating scoops of the different ice creams tightly packed next to each other on top of the crust. Smooth out the ice cream, pushing down so there aren't any empty spaces. Spoon the chocolate sauce over it. Freeze for at least four hours.

Pour the cream into a bowl. Add the powdered sugar and whip with an electric mixer until stiff peaks form. Spread the whipped cream over the top of the pie and garnish with chopped peanuts. Serve and enjoy!

LEAVE A REVIEW

I'd really appreciate it you could take a few seconds and leave a review of this book.

Thank you so much, it means a lot to me. You can leave a review at the link below ~ Dianne

http://getbook.at/REDEM

Paperbacks & Ebooks for FREE

Go to www.dianneharman.com/freepaperback.html and get your FREE copies of Dianne's books and favorite recipes immediately by signing up for her newsletter.

Once you've signed up for her newsletter you're eligible to win three paperbacks. One lucky winner is picked every week. Hurry before the offer ends!

ABOUT THE AUTHOR

Dianne lives in Huntington Beach, California, with her husband, Tom, a former California State Senator, and her boxer dog, Kelly. Her passions are cooking, reading, and dogs, so whenever she has a little free time, you can either find her in the kitchen, playing with Kelly in the back yard, or curled up with the latest book she's reading. Her award-winning books include:

Cedar Bay Cozy Mystery Series

Cedar Bay Cozy Mystery Series - Boxed Set

Liz Lucas Cozy Mystery Series

Liz Lucas Cozy Mystery Series - Boxed Set

High Desert Cozy Mystery Series

High Desert Cozy Mystery Series - Boxed Set

Northwest Cozy Mystery Series

Northwest Cozy Mystery Series - Boxed Set

Midwest Cozy Mystery Series

Midwest Cozy Mystery Series - Boxed Set

Jack Trout Cozy Mystery Series

Cottonwood Springs Cozy Mystery Series

Cottonwood Springs Mystery Series – Boxed Set

Coyote Series

Midlife Journey Series

Red Zero Series, Black Dot Series

The Holly Lewis Mystery Series

Newsletter

If you would like to be notified of her latest releases please go to www.dianneharman.com and sign up for her newsletter.

Website: www.dianneharman.com,
Blog: www.dianneharman.com/blog
Email: dianne@dianneharman.com

PUBLISHING 9/25/19

THE MONEY CLUB

BOOK NINE OF

THE HIGH DESERT COZY MYSTERY SERIES

http://getbook.at/MCLUB

A botched murder

At a very exclusive club

Chief of police – case closed

Seriously?

Marty's discovery leads her to do the "right thing," seek out the would-be murderer.

Revenge, greed, hate, love, and vices provide plenty of motives. But just which one was strong enough for someone to want to commit murder?

And what about that little Maltipoo with the wardrobe and jewels?

This is the ninth book in the High Desert Cozy Mystery Series by two-time USA Today Bestselling Author, Dianne Harman.

Open your smartphone, point and shoot at the QR code below. You will be taken to Amazon where you can pre-order 'The Money Club'.

(Download the QR code app onto your smartphone from the iTunes or Google Play store in order to read the QR code below.)

Made in United States
Troutdale, OR
07/29/2023